"IF I PLAY THE LOYAL, LOVING WIFE FOR YOU IN front of the board members, what do I get in return?"

"What do you want?" he asked.

"You may not be able to afford it."

He laughed, and she couldn't help but laugh with him.

"Try me," he said. "I'm a wealthy man."

"It doesn't concern money."

He leveled his gaze at her. "Tell me."

"I want you."

WHAT ARE *LOVESWEPT* ROMANCES?

They are stories of true romance and touching emotion. We believe those two very important ingredients are constants in our highly sensual and very believable stories in the LOVESWEPT *line. Our goal is to give you, the reader, stories of consistently high quality that may sometimes make you laugh, sometimes make you cry, but are always fresh and creative and contain many delightful surprises within their pages.*

Most romance fans read an enormous number of books. Those they truly love, they keep. Others may be traded with friends and soon forgotten. We hope that each LOVESWEPT *romance will be a treasure—a "keeper." We will always try to publish*

LOVE STORIES YOU'LL NEVER FORGET
BY AUTHORS YOU'LL ALWAYS REMEMBER

The Editors

Loveswept® 789

STILL MR. & MRS.

PATRICIA OLNEY

BANTAM BOOKS
NEW YORK · TORONTO · LONDON · SYDNEY · AUCKLAND

STILL MR. & MRS.
A Bantam Book / May 1996

ISBN 0-553-44554-5

Published simultaneously in the United States and Canada

Bantam Books are published by Bantam Books, a division of Bantam Doubleday Dell Publishing Group, Inc. Its trademark, consisting of the words "Bantam Books" and the portrayal of a rooster, is Registered in U.S. Patent and Trademark Office and in other countries. Marca Registrada. Bantam Books, 1540 Broadway, New York, New York 10036.

PRINTED IN THE UNITED STATES OF AMERICA

OPM 0 9 8 7 6 5 4 3 2

DEDICATION

To Ross
my one and only love

PROLOGUE

"I hear you're divorcing her."

Gabriel Stewart stiffened, and looked up at his grandmother, Evelyn Peters. He loosened his tie, thinking fast. He'd known it was only a matter of time before she broached the subject.

He'd also known she wouldn't be pleased.

She peered at him over the rim of her reading glasses. "I'm going to take your silence as a yes," she said. "You are divorcing Rebecca?"

Gabe let out the breath he'd been holding. "Yes."

Evelyn rose from behind her Queen Anne desk. She walked toward the window and looked out over the grounds of her Palm Springs estate.

"That's not good, Gabriel." She clasped her hands behind her back.

His insides twisted. His divorce would be final in a few weeks, and there wasn't a thing anyone could do to stop it. Not Evelyn. Not even him. Though he'd give anything if it wasn't so.

"Gabriel, the problem is that you've never known what it is that you want."

"And you do?" he asked incredulously.

"Certainly." She laughed. "I'm speaking romantically, of course. Having a couple of great-grandchildren would be nice too. You'll be a wonderful father. I don't see why you wouldn't even discuss the possibility."

A bitter taste rose in the back of his throat. "I never said I didn't want kids, only that we should wait awhile. That wasn't good enough for Rebecca."

"Yes, well, business is business," she added, her voice taking on a bored tone. "But the matters of the heart . . . ah, now that's a different subject altogether."

"And?" He knew there had to be more. With his grandmother, there always was. Something told him she was at it again. Once a matchmaker, always a matchmaker.

"I haven't made it in this man's world by being stupid," Evelyn told him. "When I see something worthwhile, I go after it." She let out a small chuckle.

Over the years, Gabe had naturally accepted his grandmother's eccentric behavior. It was, well, Evelyn. She had practically raised him after his parents divorced when he was a little boy. Once Ellen, his mother, had left for good, his father had immersed himself in running the family company, not allowing any time for his young son. Evelyn had always been there for him, and he adored her.

Now that she was in her late seventies, Gabe had thought that maybe she'd slow down. But she hadn't. Not in her personal life, nor in keeping her fingers in running the family business.

"As you know, The Toy Factory," she went on, "cannot expand into overseas operations without the support of its board members. The company is worth too much."

Way into the multimillions, Gabriel thought dryly.

"My grandfather started this company, and I intend to see it continue to prosper. Your father ran it until the day he died, and I made a good decision in making you CEO, Gabriel. You're a good businessman. You're tough when you have to be, but honest. I admire those traits in a man. But sometimes you can be rather pigheaded."

Gabe let out a deep breath. It was coming.

"I matched you with Rebecca once, and—"

"Evelyn, get to the point."

She leveled her steely gaze right at him. "The board of directors is meeting this week in Chicago with our new partners from England, Chapman and Fox."

"I know." His mind was still on Reb.

"Remember how Rebecca captivated Jonathan Fox? He's made it clear he's eager to see her again once the talks begin. The negotiations are at such a crucial stage. We need this merger to go through."

"The divorce will be final in three weeks," he said. He pushed the thoughts away. The memories of when Reb left still hurt too much.

Evelyn laughed as though it was a minor detail that didn't even deserve another thought. "Well, postpone it."

"What?"

"You heard me. Maybe you'll get lucky and win her back and start that family you know you really want. Whatever you do, do it quickly. The board and our guests are arriving in Palm Springs in a week. They want to see our operations, visit the plant. It would be nice if Rebecca was here, by your side, as your wife."

He tried to toss off the idea as a joke. After all, Evelyn had a sense of humor. Warped as it may seem at times. "You're kidding?"

"No, I'm not."

"You're a sneaky, meddling old woman. You know that?" he said, in a loving tone.

"No, I'm a romantic. I believe in true love."

"This won't work. It didn't before and it won't now," he said. "We had our differences." Plenty of them. They'd married too quickly. It was the only impulsive, out-of-character thing he'd ever done in his life. They'd married before they had a chance to get to know each other. Before they realized they were so damned wrong together.

"Right now you're still Mr. and Mrs. Put on a front until the negotiations are over. Make Jonathan happy. Afterward, I'm sure you'll do what you want. It's your business. But make it work in the time being, or we could lose everything."

She pointed a long, bony finger at him. "And you'll lose the best thing you've ever had."

Despite the persistent ache in his stomach, he knew that Evelyn would get her way.

She always did.

ONE

She was swimming in the pool.

Topless.

Even under the protective shadows of a warm spring night in Palm Springs, and clear across the wide yard, Gabe Stewart could tell.

But then some things were hard to miss, he mused. And some things, he thought again as he breathed deep of the gardenia-scented air, were even harder to change.

Like his wildly unconventional wife, Reb, for instance, who thought absolutely nothing of swimming half-naked in his grandmother's pool.

His wildly unconventional soon-to-be *ex*-wife he reminded himself.

And like how he still wanted her even though

he knew he'd be a damn fool ever to give in to the desire again.

Gabe latched the gate and walked across the wide expanse of perfectly edged lawn, across the intricate, patterned brickwork and concrete decking toward the pool.

Toward trouble.

His heart took off at a wild, untamed pace. Suddenly his mouth went dry, and his palms began to sweat. He removed his suit jacket and shrugged to loosen his taut shoulder muscles. It was way too hot, he thought, although the temperature was a balmy seventy-eight degrees. And he knew it was going to get hotter.

His gaze locked onto Reb's as she swam toward the shallow end of the pool.

She smiled at him. "Hi, stranger," she said. Her soft voice slipped around him with a distracting heat.

"Reb."

He'd forgotten just how breathtaking she was. No, Gabe decided. She was more like fire. All scorching flames, consuming white heat and blazing inferno wrapped up in one seductive body.

He wasn't surprised that he wanted her. Reb was a beautiful woman. But he was surprised that she could sap every ounce of emotional energy he had.

And she affected him the same way every time he looked at her. If he got close enough surely he'd get burned.

Just like before.

Rebecca O'Neil Stewart was his wife. At least until their divorce became final in two weeks. Contrary to what Evelyn said—or hoped for. Yet for the sake of The Toy Factory, he was going to have to ask Reb to pretend to be his happy little bride. Even though it might end up killing him in the bargain.

A soft wave of water splashed against the tiled edge of the pool. Her smile seemed to grow wider.

A trickle of sweat inched down his spine. He swore to himself.

He still had no idea what he was going to say to her. It'd been many months since he'd last seen her, since she walked out of his life and filed for divorce. They'd had a huge, ridiculous fight over vacation plans, but the real issue in their breakup had been children. She'd wanted a baby right away, but he'd said it was better to wait, since he wasn't sure if he even wanted children.

The thought of having children scared him.

After all his only role model had been his father, Charles. And Charles *wasn't* a role model.

He let out a tight breath to ease the rigid muscles around his chest, his heart, and took a step toward her.

She got out of the pool, not even bothering to reach for one of the towels nearby.

Again, he swore to himself, trying to concentrate on the deep sea-green color of her eyes.

And nothing else.

She stood on tiptoe to graze his cheek with a kiss, but he pulled back before her lips touched him.

He detected a slight hint of jasmine, the perfect aphrodisiac, lingering on the dry air. The heady aroma began to cloud his thinking.

The fragrance, clearly hers, came to him followed by other memories of their short time together. She'd been alternately wild and free-spirited, then sweet and innocent, while he had been steadily conservative and conventional. He'd wanted to take care of her for the rest of her life though Reb had made it abundantly clear she didn't need him or anyone else.

She smiled, seemingly unaffected by his rebuff.

"Where do you think you are, swimming topless?" He wrapped a thick towel around her, and pulled the ends tight. "The French Riviera or Rio?"

The greeting in her eyes contained a sensuous flame that still made his heart pound even faster in his chest.

The towel slipped down one shoulder, exposing the smoothness of her skin.

"Do you think I have any secrets left from you?" she asked, indicating her state of undress.

Gabe's muscles tightened with a sudden need that surprised him. "It's not that. It's . . . well, convention, Reb. It's just not proper."

"Oh, you mean my swimming half-naked?" Her voice turned husky and warm.

"I know I've been accused of being overly cautious," he muttered. "But you seem to think that life is just one fantasy adventure after another."

"Sorry, darling," she said. "I got the imperial summons so late. I jetted in from Phoenix as quick as I could. I hardly had time to throw a few things together. I forgot to pack a suit."

"Right."

"What else could I do?"

"Rebecca, this is hardly the time or place to be—"

"Oh, Gabe. I see you're still the same." She rubbed the towel over the top of her arms. "Conservative, stubborn." She let out an impatient sigh. "Especially when you use my full name. I'm surprised you didn't use my middle name. Unless you've forgotten it."

"I haven't forgotten." He let out a small chuckle. "And I see you're the same too, *Rebecca Ann.* In more ways than one."

She glanced at him, her gaze dancing with mischief. She turned her back and proceeded to dry the rest of herself off. "Oh, so you did notice."

He almost choked. How could he not notice?

The length of her tanned thighs stretched beyond the bottom of the towel, and the soft glow of her skin, skin that he knew would feel like satin under the brush of his fingers, certainly got his attention.

A man would have to be blind not to notice.

So he quickly looked away, telling himself that he was immune. No matter what she said. No matter what she did. She'd made it clear to him where they stood in their relationship a long time ago. She wanted one thing, he another. And nothing had changed.

Nothing at all.

She turned around, and their gazes locked. Her eyes seemed to convey a thousand messages. All of them confusing and conflicting.

But then that was Reb. And with her anything was possible.

There had been times when he'd sensed she was holding back. He knew there was something in her past that had affected her greatly. He'd often wondered if that was the reason behind her less than cautious attitude, the reason she was so adventurous.

He glanced over the top of her head and concentrated on the bubbling waterfall at the far end of the pool, the lush, green-landscaped grounds of the estate. He tried to focus on anything but the scent of Reb, or the soft curves he knew lay beneath the cotton towel.

"You look good, Gabe."

He took a step back. He knew keeping a firm distance from her was the best thing to do.

The only thing to do.

"So do you." He took in the long silk of her red hair, the twinkle in her green eyes.

"Six months is a long time for a husband and wife not to see each other," she said softly.

He tried to stop the wry smile that crept to his lips. But he couldn't. "You should have thought about that before you left. And don't forget, thanks to our quickie divorce, we have only two weeks more as husband and wife."

"I haven't forgotten. Do you remember when Evelyn first introduced us?" She changed the subject, as though talking about their divorce was as uncomfortable for her as it was for him.

He nodded. At first he'd thought it was the silliest thing he'd ever allowed Evelyn to do, to drag him into White Water Escapades, a mountain climbing and sports shop in Phoenix, Arizona. That was until he'd laid eyes on Reb.

Then it wasn't silly at all.

"And do you remember the first time we made love?" she asked.

He paused, the words stuck at the back of his throat. How could he ever forget?

"Remember how we sneaked into that tiny back room of the shop while Linda and Jim were doing inventory?"

"I . . . remember."

Rebecca laughed. She reached up to loosen his tie.

Fire sparked at her touch. The skin at his neck burned and tingled. He grasped her hand in his and slowly brought it down to her side. "Reb."

He wanted to tell her to stop what she was doing, but that was like telling himself to stop breathing.

It'd been too long since he'd seen her, felt her touch, heard her voice. She'd captured his heart in an instant with her sweet vitality and love of life. He knew within minutes of meeting her that he'd never love a woman as he did her. She was such a contrast to his very calm and controlled life.

Even now.

"And remember how we tried to be quiet but Linda kept saying to Jim, 'there's that noise again'?"

He couldn't help the smile that curved his lips. Sweetness was all he could think of. "I remember."

"I do too," she said.

Her eyes seemed to cloud over as though the memories hurt her as much as they hurt him. Reb had always been so nonchalant. Everything seemed to roll off her back.

But not now, he thought as a sharp pain pierced his heart. Right now he could see a softer, more vulnerable side to her as that old familiar protective urge hit him. Maybe he'd been a fool to let her go.

"Did you change your mind, Gabe?" She extended herself up on her toes, then down again. "Is that the reason behind the desperate phone call? Do you want to call off our divorce?"

He continued to grasp her hand in his. Heat flamed between them. He tried to ignore the blazing warmth that seeped through his skin to his bones.

Then he let her go.

"This little trip down memory lane is wonderful," he said, his voice a little rougher than he wanted it to be. "But that's not why I called you here."

He let out a deep breath and paused, considering his words carefully. "This isn't about stopping the divorce. In fact, it's quite the opposite."

"Oh."

He couldn't help but notice the sudden sadness that skirted across her features, the slight slump of her slender shoulders.

She walked toward a chaise lounge and proceeded to lay out another towel, but remained standing.

Gabe hesitated, then pulled up another chair, but didn't sit down.

"Is Evelyn all right?" Rebecca asked. "She's feeling okay, isn't she?"

"Yes, she's fine," he said quickly.

"She wanted to take a tour with me. In fact we talked about it a couple of months ago."

"My grandmother is going to be seventy-six years old in two months. She's too old to be shooting the rapids."

"She'd argue that point with you," Rebecca said, wryly. "And don't forget, Gabe, that she's my grandmother too. Even after we're divorced, I'll always have a special place in my heart for her."

"I know. Evelyn would feel the same way." He knew Rebecca was telling the truth. She'd always had a great fondness for his grandmother.

"So why did you have me drop everything? I canceled a big tour. I could have made a lot of money on that one."

Gabe took a deep breath. "I don't know why you continue to take on those tours, Reb. I told you after the divorce there'll always be more than enough money for you. I promised you that."

She smiled. "I know. But that's not good enough for me, Gabe. I want to stand on my own. I want to open my own business."

"Well then," he said with deceptive quietness. "I have a business proposition for you."

Something in his voice stopped Rebecca cold.

She let her gaze skim the full length of him, just as she had when she swam across the pool to greet him. Remembering every bit of him down to the tiniest detail. The sculpted muscles, the rock-hard legs, the warmth and the gentleness of his hands. Every single inch of his six-foot-three frame.

And with that all the memories came flooding back in one quick motion. Her search for a stable home life, including children, his strong desire to pursue his career at the expense of everything else. A sense of loneliness and emptiness filled her. As much as she tried to stop it, an image of candlelit rooms, soft music, and entwined bodies came to her.

Although the desert heat wrapped around her like a vise, she shivered. She pulled the terry-cloth towel over her shoulder, squeezing her fingers together as she tried to redirect her thoughts.

She knew it had been futile to try to banish Gabe from her heart. Seeing him now only reinforced it.

And only after months of telling herself she

didn't care, didn't love him anymore did she realize the lies she'd been telling herself.

"So what's this proposition you're talking about?" she asked as lightly as she could. "You sound so mysterious."

"Reb, sit down."

She took an even breath and settled onto the chaise lounge. She crossed her ankles, fully aware that his attraction for her was still there. She knew he wanted to touch her, just as he'd done so many times in the past. If only those feelings went to his heart.

"Okay, I'm sitting."

Somehow he seemed taller, his shoulders broader, and his hair was longer than the last time she'd seen him. She decided the length suited him. His eyes were guarded and distant.

His message on her answering machine a few days before had been pretty vague. He'd asked her to come to Palm Springs as soon as possible, and said it had something to do with their divorce. Something about a favor.

At first she'd thought maybe he'd changed his mind. But one look into his dark brown eyes had told her that he wasn't interested in any sort of a reconciliation. The emotional walls had always been there in the past, hiding his heart from her. And she suspected the barriers were still there.

Only now they seemed stronger than ever.

He turned the patio chair around and straddled it. He was close enough for her to detect the warm, heady scent of his aftershave. It reminded her of intimate embraces and soft-spoken words whispered on the edge of lovemaking. And how much he had promised to love her forever . . .

So much had changed. And not for the better, either.

She shuddered.

"Evelyn knows about the divorce," he said.

Rebecca bit her bottom lip. "I'm surprised she hadn't learned about it before now."

"She knew. Except now she's decided to voice her opinion."

Rebecca felt a smile tugging on the corners of her mouth. "Oh? So what did she say?"

Gabe playfully tapped her under her chin, sending a shiver down her neck and arms. "Don't get any crazy ideas about a conspiracy between you and my grandmother, Reb. I still have a mind of my own. And I'm not planning on a reconciliation."

She twisted a wet curl around her finger.

"Okay, so if the panic isn't about our divorce or a reconciliation, then what gives?"

He cleared his throat and she had to smile to herself, thinking this was a first. He was nervous.

"Tomorrow the board of directors from The Toy Factory is arriving from Chicago."

Rebecca pursed her lips. "Oh, I remember some of those people."

"And they remember you too."

She could feel a blush stain her cheeks.

"Some other people are coming from a company called Chapman and Fox. They have an exclusive chain of toy stores in England and throughout Europe. You remember Jonathan Fox?"

She nodded.

He clasped his hands in front of him. "We want to expand overseas, and Chapman and Fox want to hit the major cities in the U.S. To put it simply, Reb, The Toy Factory and Chapman and Fox want to put together a merger."

"There's a catch, right?" she asked.

He hesitated. "Yes, there is."

"And the catch is?"

"Evelyn thought it would be best if you were here by my side as my wife."

Rebecca stood and walked to where he sat. "Is that so?"

"It's not what you think," he said. "Evelyn pointed out that in order to pull off this merger we should put on the front of a happily married couple."

She sank into the cushioned lawn chair, her gaze focusing on the fancy brickwork at her feet. "Oh, I see."

The sudden pain of confusion and disappointment filtered through her. It wasn't as though she wanted a reconciliation either. She'd already learned her lesson, and Gabe was a good teacher. It hurt, though, that he didn't even want to try. But she was determined not to let him see what she was feeling.

"It'll be for the next ten days, Reb. Then you can get on with your life just as though I never called you. And I can get on with mine."

Under the shade of darkness, she glanced at him. "Is this what Evelyn wants?"

"Yes."

"What do you get out of this, Gabe?"

When he hesitated, she knew he didn't like any of this. In fact, she was willing to bet he regretted calling her.

"Well, for starters, my career. My position as

CEO of The Toy Factory. I've worked very hard for the past five years, and if I can pull off this merger I believe The Toy Factory will continue to grow. I want this to work. And so, I'm in complete agreement with Evelyn."

"So you want me to act as though we're still madly in love with each other. Is that it so far?"

"We can skip the madly-in-love-with-each-other part."

She frowned. "Oh, and I thought this was going to be fun."

"This isn't a game."

"That's funny coming from a man whose whole career is centered around toys and games."

"You charmed Jonathan Fox," he said. "He's looking forward to meeting you again. Jonathan is the key to this entire merger. I know he'd be terribly disappointed if you weren't here."

She couldn't help the grin that slid across her face. "Okay, if I decide to go along with this charade, that's what it's going to be, right? Just a charade."

He nodded. "Nothing more. Our divorce is still going to be final in about—"

"Two weeks."

"Well," he paused. "I have to admit the timing isn't the best."

"If I play the loyal, loving wife for you in front of the board members and Chapman and Fox, what do I get in return? I have to believe that, being the businessman you are, you wouldn't dare ask this of me without an offer in the works. Am I right?"

"Yeah, you're right."

This could turn to her advantage, she thought as wild ideas started to go through her mind. Maybe she could get what she always wanted. And Gabe was the only one who could give it to her. He was a businessman. He was used to dealing.

Only now, he was in for the deal of his life.

"I could be a hard sell, you know," she said.

It was his turn to smile at her, his eyes softening as he gazed at her.

"What do you want?" he asked.

"You may not be able to afford it."

He laughed, and she couldn't help but laugh with him.

"Try me," he said. "I'm a wealthy man."

"It doesn't concern money."

He leveled his gaze at her. "Tell me."

"I want you. Or rather a part of you."

He shook his head. "I told you I'm not interested in a reconciliation. It didn't work before.

We have different wants, different needs. We're not compatible."

"I didn't say I wanted a reconciliation."

She knew she couldn't allow him into her heart again. It hurt too much. And she'd had plenty of that to last a lifetime.

A sense of weakness shook through her before she threw it off. It didn't do any good dwelling on the past when the future suddenly looked so bright. She straightened her shoulders. Her mother had taught her the hard way that she had to be tough and not let a man like Gabriel Stewart play with her emotions.

Or her heart.

"What do you say I help you buy out White Water Escapades," he offered.

"I don't want White Water. I have something else in mind."

"Okay. Whatever. I'll give you 50K in exchange for the next ten days."

"As your happily married wife."

"Yes."

She knew it was a good offer. She needed the financial backing to open her day care center in Phoenix. She would need the stability once she started her family. The family she'd always wanted. She'd be a fool not to agree to his proposition.

But she wanted more.

And Gabe was desperate.

"I might agree to that." Reb could tell he was getting uncomfortable by the way he shifted in his chair. "But for someone with money that's too easy. So I'm going to raise the stakes a little."

He swallowed. "Okay. I'm listening."

She paused for a second and took a steady breath. What she really wanted was what had ripped them apart. Would he agree this time?

The happy chirping of crickets could barely be heard over the steady pounding of her heart.

She took a step forward. She reached up and toyed with his tie. She urged him closer to her until they were just a breath away.

"I want your child."

TWO

"You want my what?"

"A baby," she said. "Your baby."

Gabe didn't know how she moved in so close, so quickly. And without him noticing until it was too late. Too late to slip away without being too obvious.

He should have known. She was always so willing to go after what she wanted.

It was the subject of children that had put a wedge in their relationship. And that wedge, along with the strains of his job, had ended their marriage. Hadn't she learned enough then?

"Ah, Reb." His voice was almost a croak. He stepped swiftly from her grasp. "We've talked about that issue too many times in the past." He ran his fingers through his hair.

"No, we argued. We never talked." She leaned away from him. "Remember?"

She had that mischievous glint in her eyes again. Which only meant trouble with a capital T.

His stomach tightened. "I remember. But do you remember what I said?"

"You didn't want children."

"I said when the time was right we'd discuss it."

"The right time for you or me?" she asked.

"Reb, we never talked about children before we were married. Then a few weeks *after* we were married you brought up the subject. I just thought we had to slow things down a little, that's all.

"So what makes you think I've changed my mind?" he asked. "Especially right before our divorce goes through."

She watched him for a moment as though she were considering her words carefully.

"Gabriel Stewart, you're a coward."

He felt himself blush. "It's nice to know you think so highly of me."

"I always have."

He rubbed at the knot of tension growing at the back of his neck.

Reb tipped her head to the side as she watched him. In the illumination cast by the bright moonlight, he could see a kind of fascination and caring in the deep sea-green depths of her eyes.

"Don't worry so much," she said. "You've got it all wrong."

"I do?" He laughed. "You asked me for a child. I've told you I'm not ready. I don't have time to be a good father. Not now anyway."

"I'm not asking for a reconciliation. I'm not even asking that you have an active role as this child's father. I just want you to be a sperm donor so I can be artificially inseminated."

"What?" He sank back onto the chaise lounge. Was she crazy?

"It's obvious that we're not getting back together. So having sex is out of the question."

"Reb . . . I . . ."

"I want your child, Gabe. Not some stranger's. And there's no one else in my life right now."

"I need time to think about this."

She walked to stand in front of him. "You don't have time. The board is coming—"

"Tomorrow. I know."

"I want this child. And with your help, I'll be

able to start a business that will financially support my family."

"Who would take care of the baby while you're running this . . . what kind of business do you want to open anyway?"

"A day care center. It's been a dream of mine for a long time."

He never even guessed. He thought she'd always wanted White Water Escapades, not this. He swallowed, feeling guilty for not knowing his wife's dreams or seeing this side of her.

Looking back, he remembered seeing Reb at the office with the children of other employees. She'd been great with them. At the time he'd thought nothing of it.

"I'll play out your charade," she said. "I'll give you what you want if you give me what I want. What do you say?"

"I told you I need more time, that's what." He felt the hot pressure inch up his back.

"Which you don't have."

He looked away. He couldn't bear to see the pleading in her lovely eyes.

He was stuck. What was worse, she knew it. So what was more important? The Toy Factory, or the fact that she wanted a sperm donation from him?

One donation might not even take, he reasoned.

He had worked too hard and too long for this merger to fall to pieces at the last minute. Could he afford to turn her down?

"Let me get this straight," he said. "You want 50K and some of my sperm?"

"Uh-huh."

"Is this a direct deposit or an overnight drop?" he asked.

She laughed. "Do you agree?"

"Exactly what are the terms?"

She looked him square in the eye. "Overnight drop."

"I'll think about it." He knew she might be teasing him, hoping against hope to work out a reconciliation. She had to know that his conservative and responsible nature would mean they'd really have to discuss this.

So she couldn't possibly be serious.

"I need a yes or no."

"Why don't we go inside." He was over a barrel and she knew it. He directed her toward the house. "We can talk more."

"All right."

Rebecca turned her back and dropped the

towel, slipping on a T-shirt and black shorts. She picked up the towel and stepped into her sandals.

They crossed the lawn, each exchanging polite, but safe conversational tidbits, until they reached the house.

A slight figure appeared at the open French doors. "There you are, my darling," Evelyn said to Rebecca.

Rebecca wrapped her arms around Evelyn and gave her a big hug. "It's great to see you. I was outside swimming while I waited for you. How've you been?"

Evelyn beamed and winked at Gabe.

Gabe groaned. This whole fiasco would be a lot easier if he didn't have to keep an eye on the two of them. The deal with The Toy Factory and Chapman and Fox might not be worth it. Especially now with Reb's added proposal.

"Never better," Evelyn told Rebecca as they walked into the spacious living room.

The room had high-beamed ceilings, sky windows that gave an outdoor feeling, along with dozens of large potted palms and other plants. White ceiling fans whooshed overhead, sending a cool breeze across the room.

Evelyn stood back and gave Rebecca the once-over. "My, you look charming." She lifted a wet strand of Rebecca's hair, which by now had started to turn into a mass of riotous red curls. "How was the water?"

"I couldn't resist." Rebecca avoided Gabe's stare. "It was so hot, and the pool looked so tempting."

Evelyn chuckled and leveled her steely gaze at Gabe. The challenge in her eyes told him what a fool he'd been.

"I plan on using your pool a lot while I'm here, Evelyn," Rebecca said. "I hope you don't mind."

"Only if you're wearing a bathing suit," Gabe threw in as a warning.

Evelyn raised her brows at the comment. She laughed as she turned to face Rebecca. "Darling, where are your things?"

"The front foyer. Gabe's a little miffed because I forgot my swimsuit."

"Well, darling," Evelyn said to Rebecca, "if you need a swimsuit try Frenchy's over on Palm Canyon Drive. They have a huge array of unique clothes and the latest in swimwear, all designed by local artists. You'll love it."

"I'll do that, thanks."

"This business nonsense has really gotten to me, though I admit I do like playing the tycoon."

Evelyn made her way toward the wet bar. "It's a shame that's the only reason that got you here."

"It's nice to be back in Palm Springs," Rebecca said with a soft sigh to her voice. "Although Phoenix is my hometown, I still miss it here."

Evelyn poured herself a drink.

"Would you like something, my darling?" she asked Rebecca.

"Evelyn," Gabe warned softly, "Doctor Solberg said you shouldn't drink."

Evelyn waved him off. "That old coot. The only reason I still see him is to make him think I need his advice."

"You do need his advice," Gabe said. "He's supposed to make you feel better. And the doctor's orders are no drinking."

Evelyn paused for a moment then handed her drink to Gabe. "Here, you take it. I didn't really want it anyway."

Rebecca sidled up to the bar and slid onto a padded bar stool next to him. "I'd love a soft drink, if you have one."

Gabe let out a sigh and sat down. If Jonathan Fox hadn't insisted on seeing the "delightfully charming Mrs. Stewart" during the merger talks,

Gabe wouldn't be in this sticky position, sitting next to his soon-to-be ex-wife.

Nor would he be thinking of children, sperm donations, or how wonderful Reb looked, or how much she still affected him.

He watched her chatting happily with Evelyn as though they'd just seen each other the day before.

He'd forgotten what a dramatic physical presence she was with her long, untamed red curls, her tanned complexion and tall, statuesque figure. Even more, she had a way about her. Her personality caught everyone's attention, even in a crowded room.

Reb was electric, filled with fire and enthusiasm. It was one of the things that first attracted him to her. She had an innate ability to draw out of him all of the things he wasn't. Maybe more so than he wanted.

His throat constricted.

She was confident, yet fragile at the same time, he thought, taking a huge gulp from the glass of Chablis that Evelyn had given him.

"You know," Evelyn was saying, "it was the happiest day of my life when you two married."

Gabe finished off the wine in one big swallow. "Evelyn," he said as calmly as he could, "must we go into all this right now?"

He could swear he detected a hint of challenge dancing in Evelyn's gray eyes.

"Don't be such a grouch, Gabriel dear." Evelyn reached for a pack of cigarettes only to have them whisked out of her hands.

Evelyn shot Gabe a look of defiance and shrugged. "Rebecca knows exactly what's going on here. And I'm sure she knows exactly how I feel about you two and the situation in which you've now found yourselves."

Rebecca took a leisurely drink of her cola. "He told me, Evelyn."

Evelyn settled in a seat across the bar. "Well, as I was saying, it was the happiest day of my life when you two married. And equally the most unhappy day when I learned about this nasty little divorce."

"Evelyn," Gabe warned, "there's nothing nasty going on. We're just two different people who can't live together."

"Or apart," Evelyn finished for him.

She turned her attention to Rebecca. "Unfortunately, the timing of your divorce may cost The Toy Factory its merger. Jonathan Fox just simply adores you."

"I know. Gabe's told me. I'll do my part." Rebecca looked at Gabe. "And you do yours with my business . . . and your donation."

"A business?" Evelyn asked. "Donation? What donation?"

Gabe groaned silently.

"He's promised to help me open a day care center in Phoenix. It's a dream I've had for years, Evelyn. Isn't that wonderful?"

Gabe let out the breath he'd been holding.

Evelyn smiled at her grandson. "Why, Gabriel, darling, how generous of you. And smart."

"I'm doing what's best for The Toy Factory and this merger, Evelyn." Gabe shoved his hands into his pants' pockets, and wandered to the French door. His gaze traveled down the manicured lawn to the glistening pool.

He heard Reb let out a small laugh, the sound tinkling in his ears like a lost love song. Lord, help him, he prayed. It was going to be the longest ten days of his life.

"If it's okay with him," he heard Reb say.

Frowning, he walked back to where Reb and Evelyn were whispering together.

"What's going on?"

"Evelyn reminded me that the board and the

other guests are arriving tomorrow morning around eleven." Rebecca reached for his hand.

He froze. "And?"

"And there isn't enough room to accommodate all five board members and the two guests from Chapman and Fox and you and me. So . . ."

"I've had Hines prepare the guest house for you two," Evelyn explained.

"What?" Gabe practically shouted. "That small one-bedroom hideaway on the other side of the estate?"

"Of course, dear," Evelyn said. "The very same."

Gabe shook his head. "We can't do that, Evelyn."

"Why not?" Rebecca asked. "It'd be the perfect place for—"

"For nothing but trouble," he finished for her. "It won't work. We're getting a divorce. Remember? And we're not staying together, alone in that tiny little bungalow."

Evelyn poured more Chablis into his empty wineglass.

"Here, darling," she instructed. "Drink this like a good boy. And think about what you're saying. You have to make this work. A happily married couple would love to be secluded in a private, romantic hideaway."

"We'll have to think of something else." Gabe refused to look in Reb's direction. He could feel her penetrating stare boring into his back. A wave of heat fanned through him.

"Jonathan Fox," Evelyn said, "would think it's awfully strange that you two aren't sleeping in the same room. He just might think you're trying to pull something over on him. And the board is just sitting on pins and needles about pushing this merger through."

The muscle in his jaw began to twitch.

"Understand," Evelyn continued, "there is not enough room in this house for everyone."

Rebecca suddenly appeared at his side. "It'd give us time to talk."

Gabe stuttered for a reply. "I . . . ah."

Rebecca linked her arm in his, then placed a hand over his mouth. "Gosh, Evelyn, the arrangements couldn't be more perfect if I'd planned them myself."

Rebecca was delighted with the way Evelyn handled everything. She'd just won. Gabe wouldn't refuse her request now.

It was too risky not to.

She didn't know what it was about Gabe that brought out the animal in her. It wasn't that she was brazen, but pushing Gabe's buttons was just too easy.

Maybe it was the controlling facade he always wore. He'd always been passionate and loving when they were alone. That was the man she'd fallen for. She knew he was the only one she'd ever loved.

Or ever would.

Her mind drifted to happier times when he'd let himself go and have a little fun. She thought of his excitement when she proposed to do wild and crazy things to him in a crowded elevator in San Francisco. Or the time he'd stopped along the freeway during rush-hour traffic to pick her wildflowers because she'd said they were beautiful. He'd risked getting a ticket and a blemish on his perfect driving record.

She looked up at him, their gazes locking. She was certain he still loved her. Could she risk allowing him back into her heart?

Maybe he was right when he'd told her that they were opposites, and two people with values as different as theirs just couldn't live together. If so, why did she still miss him, still want him and need him?

She took in a deep breath. If she couldn't have him, at least she would have his child.

Gabe glanced quickly at his grandmother who was instructing Hines to put Rebecca's things in the cottage.

"A deal is a deal, understand?" His voice was deep and rough.

"So you'll agree to *all* my requests, then?" She stared straight at him. She wanted to leave no doubt in his mind that she was serious.

He hesitated for a second. "Yes, but only one donation. That's where I draw the line."

"Agreed."

"That means no funny stuff, either. Okay?"

"What funny stuff?" she asked.

He practically laughed out loud.

"We may be sleeping in the same guest house, but we won't be sleeping in the same bed. I'm on the couch. You can take the bed . . . alone."

His eyes said something different. She could still get to him and that pleased her.

"Whatever you say, Gabe, darling."

THREE

An hour later as Rebecca unpacked her things in the bedroom of the guest house, Gabe wandered about the small living room trying to focus on his impossible predicament. And now Reb had the advantage.

He paused by the open French door and stared out across the palm-tree-shadowed yard toward the moonlit pool. The very same pool he'd caught Reb swimming in.

He wondered if her skin was still as smooth all over. Trapped in his memory forever was the tangled flame of her hair cascading down her shoulders and across her bare breasts, and the sensuous, dangerous look in her sultry eyes.

With all her sexiness and allure, he could tell

she hadn't lost her vulnerability. She still brought out the protective streak in him.

She could steal his heart again if he'd let her.

He felt a sudden uncomfortable tightening spread throughout his tense body.

What was he going to do with her?

He heard the water from the shower turn off and then the soft tone of her voice singing in the background.

He sank down on the plump royal-blue couch and closed his eyes, refusing to think anymore. Maybe if he let his mind go numb these next ten days would be over. And when he'd open his eyes . . .

He detected the sweet scent of jasmine before he heard her walk into the room.

"Oh, there you are." Her gentle voice floated over him as softly as a heat wave.

He opened his eyes and was momentarily speechless. "What is that thing you're wearing?" The low-cut, cream-colored satin top flowed over her full breasts. Bits of white lace trimmed the edges, drawing his attention to where it shouldn't. He knew if she were to lean over, nothing would be hidden.

Her briefs came to the top of her thighs, and when she turned he could see the sides were cut clear to her waist, a waist that was made for his hands.

He jammed his fingers through his now tousled hair. The pain in his chest deepened. Lord, he wished things were different between them. "You can't wear that thing, Reb, it's too . . ."

"Too what?"

"I, ah, I guess what I'm saying is, don't you have any pajamas or a robe?"

She rolled her eyes and walked toward the small kitchen.

"My goodness, Gabe. I haven't owned a pair of pajamas in years. And I'm not going to start now just because you've suddenly turned into a prude."

"I'm not a prude."

She smiled and pulled a chilled bottle of champagne out of the refrigerator.

"I've always slept like this, remember? So what's the big deal?"

She retrieved two crystal champagne glasses from a cabinet and popped the cork. The bubbly spray shot upward, and she caught the spray in the kitchen sink.

"Gabe, don't worry so much. Everything will work out just fine," she said, drying the countertop with a towel.

"I think we should set some ground rules here for the next ten days," he said.

She carried two fluted glasses of champagne into the living room, sat down and crossed her legs.

The satin briefs inched up her thigh.

He couldn't help but notice the contrast of her tanned legs to the pale satin she was wearing.

He reached for the glass of champagne and took a huge swallow, ignoring the fiery liquid racing down his parched throat.

"For the next ten days, I'd appreciate it if you'd wear something more modest. And of course, not swim topless anymore."

"I'll get a swimsuit tomorrow, I promise."

"And some pajamas, okay?"

She rested her elbows on her knees. "You know this charade is your idea. Not mine. I can't imagine what the problem is, unless . . ."

She took a sip of champagne then placed her crystal on the pine coffee table in front of her. She smiled at him, and he knew she was teasing him.

Gabe groaned. The urge to drag her off the couch and into his arms was so intense, it was almost unbearable.

"Reb," he said after a few seconds of silence. "Please, be serious."

"Don't worry," she said, as she rose from the couch. "I won't embarrass you, Gabe. I won't ruin your chance with this merger. We both want something here. But I'm also not going to change who I am, period."

He stood to face her. "All right. Fair enough."

"Well, then." She retrieved sheets, a blanket and pillow for him. "I guess I'll be taking the bed."

He smoothed the sheet over the cushion of the couch and looked up at her.

She stood in the doorway, her soft curves silhouetted by the moonlight coming through the window behind her.

She tempted him by merely standing there.

It was almost his undoing.

"Night, Reb. Sweet dreams."

The next morning, Rebecca rolled onto her back and stretched underneath the soft floral sheets. She stared at the ceiling, and watched the slow rotation of the white overhead fan. Her thoughts were immediately drawn to Gabe.

They were both determined to carry the charade to the end, despite the difficulty of maintaining an emotional distance from each other. She knew she had to. She couldn't risk the chance of being rejected by him again if she started to depend on him as she once had.

Perhaps that's why she wanted a child so much. She'd be able to love someone unconditionally in a way her mother had never loved her. Being abandoned at age seven had taught her resiliency, but given her a tremendous fear of rejection too.

She'd never shared her shame with Gabe about being dumped in a foster home. He'd met her wonderful adopted parents, Allen and Rosemary O'Neil, but she'd never had the courage to tell him about her mother. It was too painful.

She sat up and glanced around the pale yellow and light green bedroom, breathing in the fresh scent from the assortment of bouquets in crystal vases that were scattered about the room.

Maybe if she sneaked into the kitchen without disturbing him, she could make a pot of coffee and wake him up with a steaming cup.

Rebecca silently walked out her door and peeked around the corner.

He was already gone.

She tried to tell herself it didn't matter, but she knew it did.

The fact was, Gabe had probably risen before dawn and dashed out the door half dressed in order not to see her. The sheets and blanket were folded in a neat pile to the side of the couch with the fluffy pillow on top. There was no other sign that he'd even been in the guest house at all.

She walked back into the bedroom, determined not to let Gabe spoil her joy. After all, she had the chance to get what she wanted.

A baby. His baby.

She brushed her hair up in a high ponytail, and pulled on a pair of bright red bicycle pants and a matching red sports bra. Then she grabbed her rollerblades from the closet.

What she needed to do was to work off her restless energy. Then she would shower and meet Gabe and Evelyn in the main house.

She smiled.

The morning was still young.

An hour and a half later, after circling the block for the last time, Rebecca coasted down the street, letting the rush of the air cool her steamed-up body.

The workout felt good, releasing more tension than she realized she had.

She jumped a small puddle of water on the sidewalk, rolled through the wrought iron gates and down the curve of the driveway.

Just a few feet away, Rebecca could see Gabe leaning over the open trunk of a sporty black Cadillac.

He didn't hear her approach, and as Rebecca glided closer, she was transfixed by the firm wall of his back straining through the cotton knit of his blue polo shirt. His tawny-colored shorts displayed the muscled curves of his powerful legs and she couldn't help but notice how the rich fabric stretched across his backside just right.

She grinned, soaring closer to him in one swift motion, and grabbed his butt, squeezing gently.

He hit his head with a dull thud on the inside of the trunk, and let out a litany of four-letter words.

Reb circled the car and threw her head back with a squeal of laughter.

"Rebecca, dammit." He frowned at her as she came to a stop in front of him. "You scared the you-know-what out of me." He pushed back the dark hair that had fallen over his forehead.

Never before had he looked so charming.

Then she spied the Saks Fifth Avenue bag in his hands.

"Oh, a present?" She reached for the sack only to have him snatch it away.

"Not now, Miss Nosy."

Her eyes widened with surprise. "You did get me something, didn't you?"

"Maybe."

"What is it?"

"All I can say is you can't keep wandering around in your skimpy night things," he said as he glanced at her.

She knew better than to let him slip around her heart, but the thought that he'd bought her a gift warmed her. It was the little things, such as this, that reminded her why she'd loved him so.

"Let me see, please?" she begged.

He shook his head. "This isn't the time or place, Reb."

She reached for the bag again, but he quickly shoved it behind his back.

She skated to his other side.

"I can get that, you know," she challenged.

He smiled at her. "This isn't a game, Reb. I think we should just go inside where it's cool and then I'll give this to you."

"Aw, come on. Let's see it now."

"Reb, take off the skates and come on inside. Okay?"

The businesslike attitude was back, and the wall was up again, she realized as she looked at him.

She lunged for the package, her fingers grasping the edge of the bundle. She burst out laughing as she pulled it free from his hold, and skated away from him.

Gabe leaned against the side of the car and folded his arms across his chest, clearly giving up.

She smiled at him, and surprisingly, he smiled back. Her heart jumped with new hope. "You're no fun, you know," she teased. "You could have at least given a bit of a fight."

She brushed aside her ponytail and reached inside the bag, pulling out a long, emerald-green satin robe. "Oooh!"

Suddenly she found herself blinking back tears. She looked up at him and saw the warmth in his eyes.

"Oh, Gabe. This is so beautiful. How did you ever . . . it's beautiful."

He pressed a hand to his forehead as though he was suddenly embarrassed by the whole thing.

"It's nothing. I'm just trying to keep some sense of decorum to this whole thing, that's all."

"And it's not made out of flannel or even terry cloth." She rubbed the smooth fabric against her cheek, circling closer to him. "Thank you. It was sweet of you."

"You're welcome. Just wear it, okay?" He closed the trunk and car door.

She held the robe in front of her. "It matches the color of my eyes. Did you notice that when you bought it?"

He quickly shook his head. "No, I didn't notice."

She wanted to call him the liar that he was, but she couldn't. It'd only embarrass him all the more.

She draped the robe over her shoulders and skated closer until they were barely a breath apart.

He pointed to the skates. "Where'd you get the skates?"

"I brought them with me."

"You brought rollerblades but no swimsuit."

She shrugged and skated past him. "I guess I wasn't thinking clearly."

He frowned. "Or maybe you were," he muttered. "Now, will you take those things off? The board and our guests are due to arrive soon. It'd be nice if you weren't wearing a cape like Superman and skating around on rollerblades."

"Superman's cape is red."

He laughed as she rounded the car to his left and slipped her arms around his waist. Then one skate slipped out from underneath her, and she started to lose her balance. She held on tighter, grabbing as much of Gabe as she could.

In one quick motion they were propelled across the driveway toward the lawn.

Rebecca let out a scream of delight.

Gabe's hands grasped the bare skin at her waist as she fell with a thud on the cool green grass. She rolled onto him as he lay in a dazed confusion on his back.

"Wow, that was something, wasn't it?" she asked breathlessly.

"You okay?"

"I'm okay. How about you?"

He nodded.

She was trapped by his dark gaze, but couldn't deny the hard, steady thud of her heart. Her breasts were crushed against his chest, and she wanted him to touch her. She'd been alone too long, and she saw in his eyes that he had too.

The urge to kiss him, to brush her lips across

the smoothness of his mouth called to her. The smell of him, the feel of his hard, muscled body against hers filled her senses. She felt the automatic response that was triggered just by being so close to him.

And she was acutely aware that he felt the same way toward her.

His restless hands slid down her bare back, over the stretchy sports bra to her waist. His gaze held hers, and for once she didn't know what to do, what to say.

In an instant she found herself pinned on the grass, Gabe over her and the green robe covering them like a soft canopy.

"Reb," he said softly.

The sweet sound of her name on his lips sent shivers up her arms. "Yes?"

He studied her for what seemed like a long time.

"Reb . . . Reb," he whispered again.

Then his lips softly touched hers, teasing at first as though he were tasting her for the first time. His kiss was slow, seductive. She felt the silken thrust of his tongue sweep against her lips and teeth as her mouth parted to meet him in a sensual promise of love.

She wrapped her arms around his neck, feeling the silky protection of the satin robe covering them. She felt and sensed everything that was him. His hard chest, his long, muscled legs entangled with hers, and his strong arms holding her tight.

His lips pressed harder against hers, as a rush of pure dizziness suddenly came over her.

His mouth possessed hers, devouring, tasting and sucking the sensitive inside before he stroked his tongue against hers in a primitive, sensuous way.

The approaching sound of tires coming up the drive stopped anything else he would have dared to try.

A car door slammed. Then another.

"Oh my God," Rebecca whispered.

She tugged the emerald satin from their faces, and stared up at the board members as they lined the driveway like soldiers.

And they didn't look happy.

Not one bit.

FOUR

Gabe didn't know which mistake was worse. Letting the board catch him acting like a complete idiot lying in the grass with Reb, or kissing Reb in the first place.

He struggled to get up but couldn't.

The robe was tangled between his legs and feet. The very same robe that he'd bought to keep Reb out of trouble, he realized, only made more trouble for himself.

He knew the board loved Reb and her fun-loving nature. Hadn't they hinted at that many times before? But he may have pressed his luck too far this time.

"I see you two still like to play," Marian Dorset said, her tense voice hinting her disapproval.

"Ah, Ms. Dorset." Gabe glanced up at the President of Dorset Pharmaceutical Company.

The woman stood nearly six feet tall, and her austere features were made even sharper by her hair, which was pulled back into a tight French roll.

Gabe rolled Rebecca off of his stomach. She landed on the grass with a bounce and stretched her legs out in front of her, crossing one roller-blade over the other as she glanced up at the crowd who had gathered around them.

Gabe stood and muttered an apology, then cleared his throat. "Rebecca, you remember the board members of The Toy Factory."

His gaze held Rebecca's as he reintroduced the five members in one big breath.

She smiled at them and gave a little wave of her hand.

Marian Dorset turned to Gabe. "Gabriel, you've met Mr. Jonathan Fox, President of Chapman and Fox."

Jonathan, a tall, elegant-looking man, nodded to Gabe.

"And his assistant, Mr. Oliver Bromley," Marian finished, as the younger, more stout man also nodded to Gabe in greeting.

Jonathan walked to the edge of the lawn, a

big grin creasing his face. He clasped both hands together in front of him, and bowed slightly at Rebecca. "A pleasure to see you again, Mrs. Stewart," he said, in a thick British accent.

Rebecca stood and stepped off the lawn to face Jonathan. With her blades on she met the President of Chapman and Fox eye to eye. She returned Jonathan's smile and held out her hand. "The pleasure is mine, Jonathan."

"Rollerblading looks rather fun," he said.

"The best," Rebecca agreed. "Would you like to try? We could go tomorrow morning before it gets too hot. We could get you a set of skates."

Gabe went to her side. "I'm sure Jonathan doesn't really want to go rollerblading."

"He hasn't said one way or the other." She turned to Jonathan. "Would you?"

"Maybe. Maybe," Jonathan said.

"Well," Marian Dorset exclaimed, her lack of patience plain to hear. "Let's go inside, shall we. It's getting quite hot out here."

With a twist of her hand, she gestured toward the house. "Jonathan, Oliver. Please, this way."

Jonathan turned to Rebecca and shook her hand. "My pleasure, Mrs. Stewart."

"Please call me Rebecca."

He smiled. "Very well, Rebecca."

A moment later the five board members and the executives from Chapman and Fox walked into the cool confines of the mansion.

A second of uncomfortable silence passed.

"Well, that went over pretty well." Rebecca brushed a few blades of grass from his shirt. "What do you think?"

"I'm not sure." He knew his voice showed the strain he was feeling.

Her hand lingered for a second, igniting a wild flame straight through his polo shirt. Ignoring the prickling of his skin and the crazy beat of his heart, he grabbed her hand, pushing it reluctantly away, reminding himself that he couldn't be distracted by her. Nor could he be allowed to be swept up by her charms. He had to prove to himself that he was immune to her. They had made a bargain.

Plain and simple.

But that didn't mean they would fall in love again.

"It's always the job, isn't it, Gabe?"

Stunned that she could see through him he asked, "What do you mean?"

"You're always so intense. You should lighten up a little."

"I don't know what you're talking about."

"That's too bad. For both of us." There was a melancholy shimmer in her eyes. "I hope you figure it out soon," she said. "Because until you do, I doubt you'll ever be truly happy."

She tossed the robe over her shoulders, Superman style, and skated toward the house. Gabe stood alone in the driveway, feeling like he'd just been run over by a truck.

In the marbled foyer, Rebecca set the emerald robe on the entryway table. She leaned down and took off her rollerblades.

"I say, I'm not too sure I will ever be able to adjust to this heat."

Rebecca whirled around at the sound of Jonathan's low-timbered voice. She wiped her dampened palms on the back of her shorts. "It's only started. Wait a couple of weeks and it'll blister your, ah . . ." Rebecca stopped, feeling her cheeks flush.

"This part of the country is quite beautiful," he said quickly as though he wanted to help her out of her embarrassment.

She brushed back the loose tendrils of hair that were coming free of her ponytail. "Yes, it is."

"Marriage seems to agree with you." Jonathan folded his hands together. "I'm glad to see you haven't changed. You seem as spirited as ever."

"I guess I am," she replied. "I come by it honestly."

"Jonathan, have you seen my grandmother yet?" Gabe interrupted.

Rebecca looked over her shoulder and saw that Gabe stood right behind her. She hadn't heard him come in.

He was so close, Rebecca could feel the soft fan of his warm breath against her cheek. The large foyer suddenly felt cramped, stifling. Her pulse pounded.

"No, Mr. Stewart, I have not had the pleasure just yet," Jonathan said. "I understand your grandmother will be down shortly."

"Let's go into the living room." Gabe gestured to the large room in front of them. "And get you something cool to drink. I'm sure you're thirsty after your drive from the airport."

Jonathan gave him a slight smile. "Very good." Jonathan headed toward the living room, leaving Gabe and Rebecca alone for a brief moment.

"He's a lovely man," Rebecca said.

"Uh-huh," Gabe replied a little dryly. "Coming?" he asked, changing the subject.

She made the mistake of looking into his eyes. It was impossible to miss the heat that flamed there. Why was it that Gabe could still make her feel so exposed, as if he knew her every thought.

Feeling as though her knees would buckle at any moment, she managed to pull in a ragged breath. "I suppose now is as good a time as ever to start playing out our charade," she said, unable to hide her disappointment. "I'll just run over to the guest house and change."

"Don't be long." He touched her elbow and nudged gently.

She shivered.

"Cold?" he asked as he led her to the door. "Or nervous," he finished when she didn't respond.

She slid past him and gave him a grin that she hoped would set him on fire. "Neither."

"Okay, everyone," Evelyn said in a loud voice a half hour later. "Gather around the bar, please. I have an announcement I'd like to make."

"Evelyn, is there something you'd like to tell

me first?" Gabe asked in a stern voice. He had the uneasy feeling that he wasn't going to like whatever she was about to say.

She shooed him off with a wave of her hand, but not before he saw the gleam sparkle in her eyes.

"Something we should discuss in private?" he pressed. "Like in the library?"

"No, no, no. Now stop fussing over me like I don't have a brain left in my head."

"I'm beginning to wonder," he muttered.

"Hush, before you find yourself out of a job."

Gabe rose from the couch and made his way toward the wet bar to pour himself another glass of iced tea. Maybe this uncomfortable meeting with the board would end soon so he could slip away somewhere private to nurse his pounding headache.

His gaze drifted toward Reb who was sitting between Peter Scharch, one of the more stodgy members of the board, and Jonathan. She looked crisp and cool in a yellow-flowered sundress and sandals. Not to Gabe's surprise, Jonathan Fox seemed to be glued to Reb's hip, listening attentively to every word she said.

Gabe dropped a couple more ice cubes into the tall glass. He took in a deep breath.

"Everyone, please." Evelyn waved her hands toward her guests to join her at the bar. She handed Gabe a bottle of champagne. "Gabriel, darling, open this for me, please."

Gabe popped open the bottle and poured small portions into the champagne glasses lined across the oak bar.

"I have a very special announcement to make." Evelyn handed him a glass and crooked her finger at Reb.

When Reb had joined them, Evelyn handed her a crystal glass.

"What's the big surprise, Evelyn?" Rebecca asked.

Evelyn gave her a big grin as though to say, *just wait.*

"First off," Evelyn began, "I'd like to welcome you all to my home. And I hope your stay will be enjoyable."

Murmurs of thanks to their gracious hostess floated through the living room.

"I'd also like to congratulate my grandson, Gabriel, and his wife, Rebecca, on their wedding anniversary coming up this week."

Gabe closed his eyes for a second. He should have known that Evelyn would remember their wedding date. He opened his eyes and found Evelyn staring at him, her glass raised high.

The old matchmaker was at it again.

"Evelyn," Gabe said in a stern voice.

She quickly hushed him. "Ladies and gentlemen, I'd like to invite all of you to a small party to celebrate the joy and happiness these two young people still have together after two years of marriage."

A round of applause filled the room along with congratulations.

Evelyn stared at Gabe defiantly. "Gabriel, darling, give your bride a kiss."

"Cheers," Jonathan added. "A kiss to celebrate a long-lasting relationship. For Mr. and Mrs. Stewart and our newfound relationship of The Toy Factory and Chapman and Fox."

As if on cue, Evelyn gently pushed Reb toward Gabe.

Gabe felt Reb's arm slide into the crook of his arm. He gazed down at her, and the warmth of her arm against his skin brought a strange chill of excitement to him.

Then a chill of fear.

"Cheers," Reb mimicked Jonathan, then raised her glass to Gabe's.

Crystal touched crystal.

Gabe didn't take his eyes off Reb as he swallowed the last of his champagne and set his glass on the bar.

She ran both hands up his bare arms, her deep emerald gaze never leaving his. Her skin was soft and warm. Her scent was sweet and seductive, burning a hot path straight to his heart.

Maybe even his soul.

Soft red curls framed her face, and floated across her tan shoulders. Her lips parted slightly, making his heart lurch suddenly inside his chest.

"Reb," he warned.

A slight smile skirted the corners of her mouth, but she didn't say a word.

The thrill of temptation and desire that had been surging through him since she'd arrived the night before escalated. Those feelings had nearly exploded when they'd kissed on the lawn.

There wasn't going to be any easy way out now.

Rebecca rested her hands on his chest.

Then he saw the tenderness in her eyes, and his heart melted.

He couldn't pull away.

She put her arms around his neck and in one move pulled him to her.

His eyes instantly shut.

Then their lips touched like the sweet, soft whisper of rain. Briefly and reluctantly at first.

Oh, Lord, he thought as a painful, emotional sensation swept through him like a raging fire.

Her kiss was surprisingly gentle, and pure, and he felt as though his soul had been marked forever.

Gabe slowly pulled away with only inches separating them.

He heard her catch her breath, and ecstasy spiraled through him as he realized just how much he'd missed her and remembered what it felt like to be loved by her.

A loud clap broke the sudden silence. Then another.

"Congratulations," Jonathan said.

Gasps of delight erupted from the room.

Gabe was slightly aware that the crowd of people hadn't disappeared as he would have wished. And equally aware of the lump in his throat.

Reb's eyes smoldered with the red-hot heat of desire, desire that was for him alone. Her mouth was still damp from his kiss, and he felt his resolve weaken. Gabe knew then just how in over his head he was.

"My goodness, Gabriel dear," Evelyn said.

"Are you all right? Should we call the paramedics?"

Gabe cleared his throat before glancing at his grandmother. "I'm fine."

He looked at Reb and felt ashamed of himself. He wanted to tell her that nothing had changed, that they were still incompatible.

But after that kiss, he didn't know anything anymore.

FIVE

Rebecca was sure that if Gabe's hand weren't resting on her hip just then, she would sink to the floor. She ran the tip of her tongue across her lips and imagined him touching her bare skin. The taste of him still lingered in her mouth.

For a minute she could believe that he touched her because he wanted to. Because he cared.

As he pulled his hand away and stepped back, a sudden coldness came over her. The kiss Gabe had given her was wonderful and sweet. But now Rebecca could feel that familiar wall forming around his heart.

And shutting her out.

She wanted to tell him to hold her, to continue the moment, but she couldn't.

She heard Gabe take in a deep breath of air and watched him pull himself together in that cool and controlled manner of his.

It was just as well, she thought, snapping her attention back to what was really important. She couldn't afford to get emotionally involved. She wanted a baby, his baby, and she'd get it too. But she wouldn't lose her heart again in the process.

"So when is the celebration taking place?" Marian Dorset asked.

"I've planned a gathering of thirty or forty people for this coming Sunday," Evelyn explained. "It'll be held at the Indian Springs Country Club."

Evelyn reached across the bar and patted Gabe's hand. "It'll be divine. Don't you think so, dear?"

"Yes, Evelyn. Divine." Gabe looked like he thought it would be anything but. "You wouldn't have it any other way, would you?"

"Of course not," Evelyn said.

"So, a grand celebration," Jonathan said over Rebecca's shoulder.

She turned around. "I hope you'll come."

"I've always been particularly fond of anniversaries, myself," Jonathan said. "Sentimental old fool, I suppose. In fact . . ."

As Jonathan continued, Rebecca's mind drifted to the kisses she and Gabe had shared earlier. Their wild passion had always caught them both off guard. But she had to keep her wits about her. She would be a fool to think this would lead to anything. Gabe had rejected her once before, just like her mother. But she was stronger, more independent and wouldn't let him hurt her again.

"I must tell you, Rebecca," Jonathan said. "I've never seen a couple more suited for each other than you and Gabriel."

"Do you really think so?" she asked. She glanced up and caught Gabe staring at her, hunger in his gaze. Rebecca shivered with icy anticipation. She gave him a slight smile, remembering the feel and the taste of his lips caressing hers.

And she hoped that kiss had affected him as much as it did her.

And she hoped what Jonathan had said was true.

Early the next morning in Evelyn's garden room, after too many cups of coffee, Gabe shoved the computer printouts to one side.

The columns and figures had turned into one

massive blur. He couldn't keep his mind on business and knew it was pointless to try. He had to focus on the merger plans and prepare for the meeting scheduled that morning, but he couldn't. All he could think about was Reb.

And the thoughts troubled him more than he cared to admit.

He kept telling himself the charade was only temporary, that it would end soon, but he knew he was kidding himself.

After seeing Reb again, kissing her again, he wondered if he'd ever be free. It was like she'd cast a spell on him all over again. She was irresistible.

He leaned back in his chair, coffee mug in hand, telling himself to get through one day at a time and one night at a time.

Good advice. The only problem was he wasn't sure that when this deception business was over, he'd be able to walk away from her as easily as he first thought.

He swallowed a gulp of his coffee, the taste suddenly turning bitter.

"Another cup of coffee, sir?" Hines interrupted Gabe's thoughts.

Gabe shook his head and covered his mug

with his hand. "No thanks, Hines. Do you know when my grandmother will be downstairs?"

"Not usually until nine-thirty in the morning. She wanted me to tell you to begin the morning activity without her."

Gabe shoved his mug aside. "What morning activity?"

"I wouldn't know, sir. You'd best check with Miss Evelyn or Miss Rebecca. They planned it."

With that said, Hines walked out the door.

Planned what? Gabe's stomach began to churn again. Between the two of them, trouble was most likely.

He stared at the door as though magically willing Reb to show up. He had to get to the bottom of this.

Then suddenly she seemed to appear out of nowhere.

"Good morning, Miss Rebecca." Hines followed her into the garden room.

"Morning, Hines."

"Would you like some coffee?" Hines asked her.

Reb smiled. "I'd really love a Bloody Mary. And don't forget the celery stalk."

"Certainly, miss."

Gabe let his gaze slide over her.

She wore a simple white short jumpsuit that showed off her long, tanned legs to perfection. And she looked more ravishing than he ever remembered.

Her dark red hair was woven into a tight French braid, and her large gold hoop earrings touched the curve of her neck when she turned her head.

She sat down at the glass-top table, and propped her feet on the white wicker chair beside her.

His gaze drifted to her face, to her mouth. He remembered how natural her lips had felt pressed against his just yesterday.

She looked at him with those large green eyes of hers. "Morning, Gabe."

"Morning," he murmured tightly.

"How did you sleep last night?"

She thanked Hines when he brought her the Bloody Mary.

"I slept like I always do," he answered. "We need to talk and talk now."

She took a leisurely sip of her drink. "What about?"

"Did you and Evelyn plan something this morning?"

"Yes, we did."

He frowned, making her laugh out loud.

"Goodness, Gabe. You seem to have gotten up on the wrong side of the bed, or rather, the couch."

"And fallen on my head." He leaned forward. "What the hell is going on that I don't know about?"

"Rollerblading."

Gabe started to laugh. "With Jonathan no doubt."

"No doubt. At nine o'clock," she said. "Evelyn suggested a little morning exercise, and Jonathan wants to try rollerblading."

"We have a meeting," Gabe protested.

"Now you don't." She gave him a smile. "Come with us. I told Jonathan that you personally like to check out all of the products The Toy Factory sells."

Gabe groaned. "I have a business to run. Merger plans to put together."

"Just like always. There's never any time in your life to let go, is there, Gabe?" she asked, hitting directly to the core of their problems. "No time in your busy work schedule for me."

"Don't you think this is somewhat reckless?"

Gabe still argued with her, although the idea of having a break appealed to him. "Jonathan is a little old for this, isn't he?"

"He wanted to go. He should know," Rebecca said, looking at him. "And I think it would be a prudent business move."

He laughed. "How's that?"

"It's a good chance to show Jonathan we're truly a couple." She stirred her drink with the celery stalk. "And it's an opportunity to get to know him before you start all those tedious talks."

He couldn't help but smile. "I don't know. You might get me into bigger trouble."

She let out a deep breath. "You know, Gabe, I think you can do that all by yourself."

"How's that?"

"Well, those kisses yesterday just might get me to thinking that you do still care about me," she said. "First the one on the lawn, then in the living room. I really don't know which I liked best."

"Don't get ahead of yourself. The kiss—"

"Kisses, Gabe. There were two."

He flushed. "Kisses, then. They meant nothing to either of us, so quit changing the subject.

I want to talk about this rollerblading escapade."

"But they meant something to me." Her voice was a husky whisper that sent a coil of heat ricocheting through him. "And if you can sit there and say that they meant nothing to you, you're lying." She pressed her lips to the celery stalk, then took a bite.

He tried to tell himself that her eyes weren't a lovely shade of green or that the way her pink lips parted didn't still excite him.

He swallowed. Because it did. Big time. Just as his body was proving it to him right at that moment.

"I'm telling you," he said, in as calm a voice as he could manage, "the kisses meant nothing other than that we're still human. The second one was only part of the act—"

"An act?" She laughed. "Well, you better put on a rollerblading act for Jonathan. He's expecting you. And you must be one hell of an actor, Gabriel Stewart, because those kisses were like starting a fire."

"A fire?" Jonathan asked as he walked into the garden room. "Did I hear you say something about starting a fire?"

He sat down at the table next to Rebecca.

Rebecca gave Gabe a little smile. "Tell him about the fire, darling."

"Ah, maybe later. Care to go rollerblading, Jonathan?"

"This is the stupidest thing I've ever done in my entire life." Gabe leaned over and tightened the laces on Reb's rollerblades.

"You didn't have to come, you know," Rebecca told him. "Nobody is forcing you."

He gave the bright purple laces on her skates one last tug. "That's not what you said earlier this morning."

She leaned against the wooden park table that was under a large shade tree, and gestured toward the black Cadillac. "You could get back in that car and let Hines take you home."

Gabe glanced over his shoulder and saw Jonathan pulling another pair of skates out of the trunk.

He wanted to laugh out loud from the sheer insanity of it all. He was losing every ounce of control he had left of his very controlled life.

Merger or no merger, it was crazy. And this last-minute romp through the park could just be the end of him yet.

"Not in a million years am I going to let you out of my sight."

"Now that's what I like to hear, Gabe darling." She gave him a look that practically knocked him off his skates. "You sound like you might actually start to care for me."

"I'll always care for you."

"Enough to call off this charade?"

"Let's not get ahead of ourselves," he said. "Besides, I can't let you go off with Jonathan and have him think I don't spend time with my loving wife. That's what he expects, isn't it?"

"Yep. Now there's some good thinking," she said. "And it's nice to see you lighten up a little."

"Is this how I lighten up?" He pointed to the skates strapped to his feet.

"It's a damn good start."

He reached out to take her hand but came up with nothing but air.

With a smile curving her lips, she skated backward. And completely out of his reach.

"Reb," he warned. "I'm not very good at this."

"Learn," she shouted.

"Come back here. I need—"

As the last few words escaped his mouth, his

feet slipped out from beneath him and the next thing he saw was the blue sky overhead.

The soft patch of grass cushioned the blow to his head. He let loose a few well-chosen words, only to bring Reb to his side.

"Gabe, are you all right?" She came to a fast stop with a turn of her skates, her voice full of panic.

She fell to her knees beside him and touched his face, his arms, shoulders.

"I'm all right." He pulled himself to a sitting position, feeling various parts of his body already beginning to ache.

"I don't know what I'd do if something happened to you," she said quietly. "Maybe you shouldn't be doing this after all."

He cupped his hand against her cheek, then smoothed back a few loose strands of red hair. She leaned closer to him and touched her lips to his.

At first the contact was light, teasing, then grew more demanding as he pulled her closer to him.

"Er-hem."

Rebecca moved away from Gabe at the sound behind them.

"Are we skating this morning?" Jonathan asked. "Or do we have a different agenda?"

Rebecca stood. "Gabe took a little fall."

"So I see. Are you injured? Should we call for help?"

Gabe shook his head. "No sir. I'm fine." He looked at Reb, and her gaze turned soft when he smiled at her.

"My ego is bruised, that's all."

"Very well," Jonathan said. He gave Rebecca a wink and skated away.

Several hours later, Rebecca returned from her shopping spree at Frenchy's. As she slipped past the closed library doors, she could hear the muffled voices coming from the other side.

She paused for a second, knowing it wasn't right to listen, but she couldn't help herself. She heard Gabe's deep voice, then Marian's. She didn't fail to catch Jonathan's heated and disapproving tone. She frowned. The talks didn't sound like they were going very well.

"Eavesdropping, dear?" Evelyn said behind her.

Rebecca whirled around, her hand at her throat. "Evelyn, you scared me."

Evelyn raised her brows. "I suppose I did. But that usually happens when people are caught doing something they probably shouldn't." She smiled and patted Rebecca's hand.

"Things aren't going too well, are they?"

Evelyn shrugged. "All this nasty business stuff."

"Anything I can do to help?"

"Putting an end to this divorce would be a start. Although a real kick in Gabe's pants would do the job much better."

"Oh, Evelyn." Rebecca laughed. "I meant with the negotiations. What's the problem?"

Evelyn waved her hand in the air. "The recent drop in sales are making the talks more difficult. It bores the heck out of me. That's why Gabriel is in there instead of me. I'm getting too old for all of that."

"You'll never be too old, Evelyn. Why don't you go for a swim with me. I bought myself a suit." She indicated the bag from Frenchy's.

Evelyn turned Rebecca away from the library, looping their arms together.

"That sounds wonderful. Then perhaps you and I could talk about what we can do with this stubborn grandson of mine."

"I couldn't agree with you more," Rebecca said and followed Evelyn up the stairs.

After being sequestered in the library for most of the afternoon, Gabe felt drained and tired.

Fox was driving a hard bargain, one that The Toy Factory needed to accept even though the board couldn't see it yet. Their discussions—arguments, really—would continue during dinner at the Indian Springs Country Club.

Minutes after everyone left for a tennis match at the club, Gabe headed straight for the bar. He spied Evelyn making her way up the stairs, noting that she'd been outside swimming.

He pulled out two soft drinks, and walked outside to the pool.

He stood for a moment, taking a huge swallow of his drink, not surprised to find Rebecca lounging on her back on a bright yellow float, like a satisfied, pampered cat.

In fact, he'd hoped she'd be there.

"The water looks good," he said, thinking how beautiful she was.

Rebecca smiled and stretched. She slid off the raft and glided through the shimmering water to where he stood near the edge.

"Why don't you join me?"

"Why don't you join me for a drink, instead?" He showed her the cold can.

Her brows lifted above her dark sunglasses. "That's the nicest offer I've had all day."

She stepped out of the pool to stand inches from him, and for the first time Gabe noticed her new bathing suit.

He took in a sharp breath of air.

The one-piece suit was emerald green and hugged every curve of her body. The back dipped low and was cut high on the hips.

Gabe took a swallow of his drink, trying to push the memories of her naked body in his arms out of his mind.

"I'd like something cold to drink. Thanks." She took the can from him, and their fingers brushed for a second.

She walked toward a chair, giving him a closer look at how perfectly she filled the bathing suit. The sweep of her tanned back, the gentle sway of her trim hips sent a surge of arousal through him.

He walked toward her, and she turned swiftly around. The sun's rays flashed against the fiery-red of her hair. The curls, now unbound from her French braid, fell across her shoulders in soft waves. She removed her sunglasses and placed them on the table.

The emotion he saw in those green depths moved him. For a split second he wanted to touch her, run his hands down the curve of her spine, feel the smoothness of her skin. He wanted to grab her to him and kiss her until she was dizzy. Until she begged him to stop.

"Hard day at the office?" She raised the can to her lips and took a drink.

He took her hand in his. "Couldn't be worse," he whispered, more intrigued at the soft feel of her skin against his.

"Remember how I would massage your neck and shoulders when you had a tough day?"

He nodded, remembering how the touch of her skilled fingers along his tense shoulder muscles would put him in another dimension.

"It's amazing how you always seemed to know when I needed that little extra attention to make my day easier. It's as though you possessed some sixth sense."

"It comes when you truly care for someone, Gabe."

"I suppose I should have told you this when

we were married," he said, "but I really appreciated all that you did for me. Always putting my needs before your own. Maybe it would've helped us if I'd acknowledged that then."

"I could do it now for you if you want," she offered in a soft voice.

Without waiting for his reply, she put her can of soda down and then his. She nudged him onto a lawn chair and stood behind him, gently rubbing and kneading his shoulder muscles.

"Just relax for a few minutes." She ran her fingertips underneath the cotton of his shirt. "Forget all about those awful merger talks."

"Why are you so good to me?" he nearly groaned as her hands manipulated his tender flesh.

Despite the heat, he shivered.

Without thinking, he grasped one of her hands.

He turned his head and their gazes locked.

She raised his hand to her lips and kissed him ever so slightly. "That's why," she murmured, rubbing his knuckles across her lips.

Everything around him seemed to disappear. Except her.

"Does that help?" She closed her eyes.

"Tremendously," he replied, taking in the sweet scent of her. "It always did."

God, how he wanted her.

He stood and pulled her to him, feeling and remembering how perfectly she fit inside the junction of his hips. He dropped his hands to her waist, squeezing softly. Then his hands roamed over her back, exploring gently, but filled with promise as a fire started to rage inside him.

A sharp emotion went through him of just how foolish he was. He knew he shouldn't be doing this. He, who focused so much on what was right and tried to honor his obligations above all else, was taking a very destructive path. This would just lead to more heartache for both of them.

But the truth was, she had too much power over him.

Her hands went to the open collar of his shirt, her fingers touching the hair at the base of his neck.

A shot rippled up his back.

She arched her neck, and he ached to touch his lips to her skin, ached to feel everything about her.

He groaned involuntarily.

"Wasn't there something about starting a fire?" she murmured.

"More like a raging inferno," he whispered, knowing he should be pulling away.

"Well, set me on fire, Gabe."

SIX

Rebecca felt as if she were falling into a bottomless pit.

Gabe's strong hands circling her waist, caressing her back were even better than she'd remembered.

A sigh escaped her lips.

He grasped her arms in his hands and brought them close to his chest, wrapping her in his warmth.

Then he briefly touched her lips with his.

She struggled to take in a deep breath, bringing into her senses everything that was him. The soft touch of his mouth, the sweet taste of his tongue, the smell of him, clean and masculine.

She hoped the moment would continue forever.

"I dreamed about you last night," he whispered.

She opened her eyes and focused on him, his chiseled features, his soft mouth, his dark eyes.

"I'm surprised it wasn't a nightmare."

He gave a deep, throaty laugh. "In fact, it's becoming nearly impossible to stop thinking about you."

She touched her bottom lip with the tip of her tongue, aware that his gaze followed her movements.

"What do you say we order pizza for just the two of us tonight? We can share a quiet evening, you and me. Alone."

Without any warning at all, his demeanor changed. He squeezed her hands as he tensed.

"As tempting as that sounds, I can't."

Much too quickly, she felt her smile dim, and her hopes sink.

"I have a dinner meeting at the country club."

"Tell them you're busy," she said matter-of-factly.

"Ah, Reb." His voice took on that cool tone she hated. "I can't."

The emotion and love she'd seen in his eyes moments before were suddenly gone, replaced by the serious look she'd seen far too many times. It was as though they'd pushed each other too far, and Gabe was the first one backing off.

Running away was more like it.

She stiffened more with hurt than anger. "Sounds like you won't."

He brought her hand up to his mouth. "Dammit," he swore, pressing his lips to her open palm. "Please be reasonable."

"I'm trying. Really I am."

"I want this merger to go through more than you can imagine."

"Why?"

"Because the company is slipping."

She took in a steady breath, amazed that he actually admitted something was wrong. He'd never opened up to her about anything when they were together.

"Jonathan has made an offer that the board thinks is too low," he continued. "This is my family's company we're talking about. I don't like being forced into a corner."

She'd learned that lesson the hard way. She'd forced him into a corner once before and now they were headed for a divorce.

"What about our agreement? The baby? We need some time to discuss it."

"I can't deal with this right now." He sounded impatient. "Make an appointment with my secretary the first Monday after this whole mess is over. I promise we can discuss all the tiny details."

"Fine, I'll get in touch with your secretary." She slipped her feet into her sandals and wrapped her towel around her waist.

"I'm sorry." He grabbed her hand. "I don't mean to act as though I don't care about what you want. You've been more than generous with your time and everything else. You don't know how much I appreciate it. But this merger has to be my first priority. You understand?"

"Maybe if you'd spent even half as much effort fighting for our marriage as you are fighting for your company, we wouldn't be in this situation."

She headed toward the guest house, knowing he was watching every step. She looked over her shoulder, having at least a little satisfaction in seeing that she was right. He looked about as bad as she felt.

"I hope you get what you want, Gabe," she said, and walked into the house.

Gabe saw Reb the instant he walked into the garden room the next morning. She was sitting with Evelyn and Jonathan sharing a breakfast of eggs Benedict and fresh squeezed orange juice.

After their encounter by the pool, Reb had tried to stay out of his way, avoiding his looks and even his attempts at small talk every time they saw each other.

After morning greetings were exchanged, Gabe sat down, his gaze focused on Reb. He poured himself a cup of coffee, and waved aside the plate of eggs Hines brought him.

Every single nerve was on an all-stage alert where Reb was concerned. Every emotion that surfaced, he tried to smother. Every urge, right or wrong, he forced back down until he thought he would go crazy with it all.

He knew she was right. He had let work interfere with their relationship, but running his family's company was what his whole life had been about. He'd worked too hard not to give it his all. Unfortunately, he hadn't had enough left over to give their relationship the time and attention it needed. And ultimately their irresistible attraction for each other hadn't been enough. They needed so much more to base a lifetime on.

Especially with two people as different as they were.

Gabe took a swallow of his coffee, noticing he'd let the drink go cold on him. Shoving the cup aside, he glanced across the table.

Jonathan was deep in conversation with Reb. She glanced at Gabe and then quickly back to Jonathan when he said something that made her laugh.

Gabe felt his insides contort with jealousy. Why now, of all times, just a week before their divorce would be final, would he be feeling the pangs of loss?

Jonathan turned to him. "Gabe, Rebecca's just been telling me about the day care center she plans on opening."

Gabe smiled in acknowledgment and tried to put on a good front.

"I'm impressed with some of the wonderful ideas she has," Jonathan continued. "Fund-raisers, special activities for handicapped youngsters involving the community and business people. It's a wonderful advertisement for the company. You can count on me to donate whatever sum is needed to help this worthy cause get off the ground."

"Thank you, Jonathan," Gabe said.

Evelyn patted Gabe's shoulder. "I'm so happy everything is working out so well. Don't you think?"

Gabe grunted.

Rebecca smiled brightly at Jonathan, avoiding Gabe's eyes. "So what are the plans for today? If you'd like to sight-see, Jonathan, there are Jeep tours, or the aerial tram."

"Sounds interesting."

"There's also parachute jumping," Rebecca continued. "Now that's a lot of fun."

"Rebecca, dear," Evelyn interrupted. "Let's keep Jonathan on the ground where we need him."

Once Hines removed the plates from the table, Evelyn leaned toward Gabe. "You should take thc afternoon off, dear. You look a little tired. Are you getting enough sleep?"

"Enough to get by," Gabe murmured before looking over at Reb. Their gazes locked and held for what seemed like an eternity.

"I've planned a round of golf for everyone." Evelyn nodded to Jonathan. "And Jonathan has agreed to postpone this morning's meeting until late this afternoon. Isn't that right, Jonathan?"

"We need a break," he said. "And I'd like to

refresh my golf game. Though that parachute jumping sounds rather exciting."

Evelyn laughed. "Good. It's settled."

"Evelyn," Rebecca said, "do you need another player to even out the set? I'd love to play."

Evelyn shook her head. "We have two groups of four, including myself. Why don't you and Gabe take the aerial tram and have lunch on top of the mountain?"

"That's a wonderful idea," Rebecca said. "What do you think?"

Gabe hesitated, knowing that everyone was listening and waiting for his answer.

He tried to remind himself that being alone with Reb was dangerous, but at that moment he didn't care.

"I could use a break."

"Wonderful," Evelyn said, her voice full of victory.

Rebecca sat on the chintz-cushioned chair in the front foyer, tapping her sneakered foot on the marbled floor. She'd been waiting for Gabe for what seemed like eternity.

In that instant, Gabe rounded the corner and

stopped down the hallway from her. For a brief second they watched each other.

In one hand he held an open straw basket, and under his other arm was a large blanket. His hair was still damp from a shower, and she had the urge to feel the thick texture between her fingers.

She swallowed.

He squared his shoulders and walked toward her.

She held her breath for a second. She could see his muscles ripple beneath his gray knit shirt and jeans.

"Did you want lunch?" He held up the straw picnic basket.

"Oh, that's a great idea. Thanks for remembering."

He eyed the cropped red top and denim shorts she wore. "Only shorts? It might get a little cool on top of the mountain."

"You'll keep me warm."

He arched a brow at her comment. "It's a public place."

"Since when did that ever stop you from putting your arms around me in public?"

He smiled.

"Seems to me," Rebecca went on, "that

you've done a lot more than just holding me in public."

"Kissing isn't a crime," he reminded her. His gaze held a warning that unnerved her. "Do you have a sweater or something?"

"I have a sweatshirt." She indicated the large bag at her feet, then took the picnic basket from him. Their fingers brushed and passion grew in her heart like a song. "Why the wine?"

He shrugged.

"Are you planning to seduce me?" she asked in a sweet voice, feeling the warmth of his hands. "To woo me on top of the mountain over a bottle of wine?"

"Are you looking for trouble, Reb?" His voice showed signs of interest.

"Depends, Gabe." She suppressed a tiny moan at the back of her throat. "Are you offering?"

"That's the last of the rosé." Gabe handed Reb her half-filled glass.

It had been almost two hours since they arrived at the aerial tramway, traveled the three and a half miles up the hill, eaten the lunch Hines had packed for them, and taken a small hike along one of the many tree-lined mountain trails.

"We really finished that bottle off quickly, didn't we?" Rebecca sipped the last swallow.

She placed her glass inside the straw basket along with the other picnic items. Gabe leaned back and stretched his legs out on the blanket, watching her. Under the shade of a huge evergreen, he had the unobstructed view of the Coachella Valley below, the San Jacinto mountains behind him, and Reb right beside him.

And he'd never seen anything more lovely in his whole life.

She'd loosened her hair, allowing the thick waves to lay across her shoulders. He wanted to wrap his fingers around each wild curl and inhale its clean, sweet scent.

"Why didn't you tell me about the day care center when we were married?" Gabe asked.

She brushed her hair aside but didn't look at him. "You were always too busy."

Again, he'd failed her. It was as though he'd turned into his father. Always working. Never having the personal time for his family. A bitter feeling of resentment churned deep in his stomach.

Awkwardly, she cleared her throat. "I didn't want you to think it was a silly idea."

He touched her hand. "I don't think it's silly."

She shrugged.

"Reb. Why the desperate need for kids when we'd been married for such a short time?"

"Because it's the only way I can fill this empty place inside me, Gabe. I love children."

"Wasn't I enough? Didn't I make you happy?"

"Yes, I loved you. You made me very happy." Her voice trailed off.

"But not completely," he added for her. "Otherwise we wouldn't be having this conversation." He stretched back, resting on his elbows. "You know, I always had this feeling you never needed me. At least not in the way I wanted you to need me."

"Really?" The shock in her voice was plain to hear.

He nodded. "Yeah, you were always so strong and independent. You remind me a lot of Evelyn in that way."

"Gabe, I—"

"Reb, do you remember why we broke up?"

She blushed a light pink. "We had this huge, stupid argument."

He sensed she was stalling, but then she continued.

"I remember you had to plan out our vacation to the tiniest detail, the hour, the minute, pinpointing each and every thing we were going to do. I felt like a business meeting, not a wife."

"I wanted to give you the best."

"You didn't have to. It was as if you were trying to buy my love. As if just being with me wasn't enough for you."

He felt a heavy twinge of regret and emptiness. "I didn't want anything to go wrong."

"Life has no guarantees. Just like in business, you take risks. You should know that."

"But in business you have more control if you plan carefully."

"Life can't always be controlled."

"This is crazy." He shook his head. "And so were those arguments. It wasn't just the arguments that broke us up. They were a symptom of bigger problems." A stab of sadness went through him as he thought about all they had lost.

He sighed. "You are the most exciting woman

I've ever known. I want you to know that. I will treasure the memories forever."

He paused for a second, seeing only the bittersweet desire in the depths of her eyes.

"Since that argument, I've had a lot of time to think about things," she murmured. "We both said a lot of hurtful things, Gabe. I want you to know that I made a mistake by threatening to divorce you. It was supposed to be a wake-up call. I didn't think you'd take me up on it."

He swallowed the lump that suddenly had formed at the back of his throat. "It was a dangerous argument that backfired."

"I know."

"You hurt me, Reb. I lost all the trust I had in you. I can't ever be sure you wouldn't do it again."

"I know you tried to give me everything," she said, hesitation clear in her voice. "When you stormed out that night, it reminded me of my mother . . ." She struggled for the words. "When my mother abandoned me at the foster home."

"What are you talking about?" he asked. "I thought Allen and Rosemary adopted you when you were a baby. You never mentioned any foster home."

"I never liked to talk about it."

He lifted her chin to meet his gaze. "Why couldn't you tell me?"

"I didn't want you to feel sorry for me. I was supposed to be strong. That's what, Teri, my biological mother, always told me to be. I'm tough, you know." She straightened her shoulders with false bravado.

He ran his fingers down the side of her cheek, lingering at the corner of her mouth. *No, you're not tough*, he wanted to tell her. *You're sweet and gentle and oh, so fragile.*

"How old were you?"

"Seven."

He sucked in a breath. "Sweetheart, I'm so sorry." He shook his head. "I'm stunned, shocked."

He stared out into the distance. He'd experienced some of the same things as a child. Things he'd never told Reb about either. Technically his father hadn't abandoned him as Reb's mother had. But the pain of being sent away to boarding school felt the same.

Gabe's chest tightened as the resentment surfaced. The need to hold her, tell her everything would be all right overwhelmed him. "Is this why you want children so desperately?"

She nodded. "I wanted to make sure I was doing this for the right reasons, so I went to some adoption seminars. I even talked to a psychotherapist."

"So you're sure."

"Yeah, I'm sure. My heart and soul are screaming for me to do this, Gabe."

"I wish you would have told me about this sooner, Reb. At least then I'd have been able to understand you better."

"When you walked out after that fight, all those horrible memories came flooding back. I couldn't stop thinking about them." Her voice drifted into a hushed whisper.

"Reb," Gabe said softly. "I can't begin to tell you how bad I feel about what happened."

She leaned closer to him. "It's in the past where it belongs."

He touched her cheek, stroking upward to cup her face. Then, through a hazy veil of passion, he instantly wrapped her in his arms.

Slowly, he lowered his head to kiss her.

Their lips brushed, touched, and tasted.

Then the fire started.

SEVEN

Rebecca gasped at the feel of Gabe's chest as he lowered her to the blanket. His kisses intensified and grew harder and more demanding. His mouth devoured hers, leaving her burning with unchecked desire.

Like a sculptor, his hands found the exposed skin of her back where her top had inched upward. His fingers molded her skin, then stroked her with a featherlike touch, sending a blazing streak of heat up and down her spine. His grip tightened.

He muttered something against her lips, and she opened her mouth for him, allowing his tongue to probe and twist with hers.

He tasted wonderfully sweet, the nectar of the rosé still lingering on his tongue.

He rubbed his hand along the slim curve of her hip, pulling her closer to him. She nestled her thigh between his legs, drawing a deep moan from him.

Pressed together, she couldn't help but notice the state of his arousal, his desire for her. Her hand traveled down to the metal buttons of his jeans. Cupping him lightly at first, she began to massage him through the rough fabric.

He groaned low in his throat, the sound luring her closer.

She slipped one button on his jeans free. Then the next. And the next.

She wanted to touch him, to feel the smooth hardness of him. She slid her hand under the stiff material of his jeans until her fingers grasped and held him gently.

He mumbled her name against her ear, his lips burning a sizzling path down her neck.

It was as if they'd never been apart. Their passion for each other was urgent and wild, out of control.

Then something made him stop and pull away.

"What . . . ?" she breathed in shock at the sudden void. "What's the matter?"

The wall was up again. He'd lost the control he treasured so much. She saw it in his eyes.

"I'm sorry." His smoky voice was a mix of excitement and strain. He leaned back, quickly buttoning his jeans.

She felt something tighten inside of her. "So am I."

Rebecca shot straight up in bed, her hand at her throat. She was sure she heard something.

Despite the breeze from the ceiling fan, a bead of perspiration inched down her spine. Through the partially parted shutters, she could see it was still dark. She checked the clock on the nightstand.

It was almost three in the morning.

She crawled out of bed, slipping on the cool satin robe that Gabe had bought her. She walked toward the door, a stream of moonlight guiding her way. She peeked around the corner expecting to see Gabe in the living room in his usual spot.

To her surprise the small couch was empty. The blankets were crumpled in a heap in one corner of the sofa, and the once fluffy pillow was now squashed and lying limp on the floor.

The French door creaked open with a yawn.

She whirled around, realizing the door hadn't been closed all the way. She walked to the door intent on shutting it but then she stopped.

The moon, now full and hanging high in the night sky, beamed a full light across the lawn and the pool.

There, silhouetted in the shadows, stood Gabe.

He was bare-chested, wearing only a pair of shorts, his hands shoved in the pockets. He stood motionless, staring into the water as though he was hypnotized.

Her throat tightened. Hot tears filled her eyes. She furiously wiped them away with a swipe of her hand.

Slowly, she turned, latching the door shut behind her.

Damn him, she swore.

She knew he was fighting. Fighting her, himself and their unbearable need to be near each other.

She walked back into her bedroom and slipped into bed, pulling the sheet up to her chin. They both had lost so much already. She wasn't willing to lose anymore. Was she strong enough to fight for them both?

The next evening, Rebecca and Jonathan were in the kitchen making a colossal sundae—and a big mess.

"Here are some cherries, Jonathan." Rebecca shut the refrigerator door.

"Excellent, my dear, excellent."

She opened the jar and plopped a couple of red cherries on top of the chocolate-covered ice cream already decorated with whipped cream and chopped nuts.

Rebecca climbed on top of a bar stool and picked up her spoon.

"This is very good." Jonathan glanced up at her. "I like your style, Rebecca."

She smiled. "Thank you."

"Your husband, he is more . . ."

"Conservative?" Rebecca finished for him.

Jonathan scooped a large bite into his mouth and nodded. "He worries too much."

"I know."

"I see a lot of myself in Gabe. Like him, I was intent on being the best, and working hard.

"I didn't realize how unbalanced my life was until my wife made me choose." He rested the bowl on his lap. "Arlene finally told me it was her and our children or the business."

"What happened?"

"My priorities changed. It was either that or my home address, according to Arlene."

Rebecca laughed. "You tell wonderful stories, Jonathan."

"I hope to make a point here. I was stubborn. Just like your husband. But Arlene was more so and let me know it."

"Reb?" Gabe said from the doorway. "Oh, I didn't know you had company." He walked in, looking at the mess spread across the kitchen.

Jonathan stood and put his half-eaten ice cream on the counter. "This was delicious. But I must watch my weight. Thank you, Rebecca." He gave her hand a slight squeeze. "Until tomorrow night. I'm looking forward to your party."

Rebecca sighed as she watched Jonathan leave.

"What was that all about?" Gabe asked.

"Actually, we were talking about you." She took a bite of ice cream, slowly licking the spoon.

"What did he tell you?" His pupils dilated, turning his eyes an even darker shade of brown.

"That you work too hard. Just like he did until his wife told him enough was enough." She ladled another spoonful of whipped foam and strawberry ice cream. "Want some?"

When he shook his head, she took a bite. He looked so handsome, it made her chest hurt. She popped a cherry into her mouth and chewed, knowing that somehow, somewhere she'd lost her will to resist him. And she didn't know what to do.

Forcing her heart and mind away from him, she went to the kitchen sink intent on cleaning up the mess scattered across the counter.

"Here," he said, his voice low as he took in a shaky breath. "Let me help."

She turned abruptly and ran directly into him. Gabe stumbled backward against the butcher-block island, knocking over two bar stools. He grabbed her around the waist and pulled her hard against his hips. Rebecca let out a gasp as a third chair toppled over with a bang.

"That's not necessary," she said softly, her gaze taking in the open V of his cream-colored shirt, the warmth of his eyes. "We made the mess. I can clean it up real fast."

He made no effort to hide his obvious hunger for her, and in that instant, she knew Gabe was changing, softening.

Glancing down, she noticed a button of his

shirt was caught in her cotton sweater. She grabbed at the front of her sweater to stop him. "Don't move, you'll tear your—"

The sharp sound of ripping material filled the air.

She glanced down at his torn shirt. "Looks like we've had a little accident."

"Nothing is little where you're concerned."

Unable to help herself, she ran her palms over the smooth, hard curves of his muscled chest to where the button of his shirt was connected with her sweater. "Now hold still." She pulled the button free. "I want to untangle us."

"I don't." His voice was rough and deep.

Placing his large hands on her face, he tipped her chin up and kissed her. He eased his tongue into her mouth, causing her to draw in a ragged breath. He captured her tongue with his lips, sucking gently.

She moaned as he devoured her, suddenly so aroused, he could have taken her right then.

But would he? Would he let down his guard and make love to her?

Would she let him?

Before she could even form an answer, Gabe stiffened.

"Oh, no, Gabe," Rebecca whispered. "What's wrong?"

To her dismay, she saw Hines standing in the doorway.

A trace of a smile showed around Hines's mouth. "Er, um, excuse me, Miss Rebecca. I'm sorry to disturb you. But Miss Evelyn needs to see you right now. She's waiting in her bedroom suite."

"Tell Evelyn I'll be right there."

Hines nodded and walked out of the room.

Rebecca looked over at Gabe who was picking up the tipped over bar stools.

She pushed back her hair. "Evelyn's waiting," Rebecca said hesitantly as she walked toward the door.

She saw a spark of some indefinable emotion in his eyes, a smoldering fire. She couldn't be sure exactly what it was.

She just wondered if she'd ever get the chance to find out.

"Your dress for the party arrived from Frenchy's," Evelyn told Rebecca. "Just a short while ago."

"You peeked?" Rebecca inspected the beaded

dress that hung on its hanger near the closet door.

"Of course. I couldn't help myself. I wanted to be sure you were on the right path to seduction. I hope you don't mind."

"Seduction?" Rebecca pulled the plastic cover back over the dress.

"Yes, seduction. And I'm pleased to say that you have chosen wisely."

"Thank you."

Evelyn sat curled up on an overstuffed chair, her reading glasses perched low on her nose. "You're welcome. At least you have good taste."

"Evelyn, what are you up to?"

"Why do you think I suggested you go to Frenchy's in the first place?" She tossed the book she'd been reading to the floor. "That sinfully delightful bathing suit worked. Didn't it?"

"Evelyn, have you been spying?"

"I'm old, but I still have my ways." A small smile lifted the corners of her mouth and then it disappeared.

"You know after you moved back to Phoenix he closed the big house you two lived in and moved into the Cypress Street condo," Evelyn said.

"You must be glad he's close by," Rebecca commented.

"Yes," Evelyn said. "Gabe has always taken care of me ever since Max, my last husband, died so many years ago. But lately he's starting to bother me. He's such a mother hen."

Rebecca could only smile at the thought.

Evelyn sighed. "He closed that house because of the bad memories, you know."

"No, I didn't know."

"He didn't say much about it, but I could tell. He's not as clever at hiding his emotions as he thinks he is. But he's been like that ever since he was a young boy. Very serious. But my son was too. Charles, Gabriel's father, was all work, no play. He taught Gabriel a strong code of ethics, but without much affection. I think it pushed Gabe too far. And then there were those boarding schools."

"What schools?" Rebecca felt her heart sink.

Evelyn blinked and then looked at Rebecca as though seeing her for the first time. "That's where I went wrong. I should have stepped in and told Charles that with a sensitive little boy like Gabriel, being away from home all the time would be too much. But I was too soft on Charles as well."

"When did Gabe go to boarding school? And where was his mother?"

"Oh, she was long gone the minute the divorce was final. Said she wasn't cut out to be a wife or a mother. Gabriel went to boarding school soon after. He was very young at the time. Ten, I think. Charles was never very demonstrative, and the divorce . . . well, I shouldn't have to tell you that it wasn't good. Especially to that young boy. He was devastated by it all."

"Poor Gabe." Rebecca had never known any of this. Maybe she and Gabe weren't that different after all.

Evelyn wiped her steel-gray eyes with a tissue. "Poor Gabe, hell," she said, her voice rising. "He survived. We all do. And so we'll just have to change him. That's all."

"Oh, Evelyn." Rebecca laughed. "You are terrible, you know that?"

"I saw the two of you out there cozying up by the pool. That was a good start. Then nothing. What is the matter with you two anyway?"

"Ask your grandson." Rebecca picked up her dress.

"I intend to."

Rebecca walked toward the door.

"Who knows, Evelyn," Rebecca said, "maybe

a plan of seduction is the way to go. And perhaps this dress is the right start."

"Damn," Gabe whispered as his gaze swept the silvery vision of his wife standing in the doorway of the banquet hall at the Indian Springs Country Club.

"What's that, Gabriel, dear?" Evelyn asked.

"Nothing." He signaled a waiter carrying a tray of drinks. He grabbed a glass of white wine as Rebecca walked straight toward him.

The silver-sequined dress she wore sculpted her body perfectly. It came to her midthigh, giving a provocative view of her long, curvy legs. The tantalizing neckline, with its spaghetti straps, pulled tightly across her full breasts.

Her high-heeled silver sandals made her seem taller, and when she turned to accept a glass of wine, Gabe noticed the dress dipped low in the back to her waist.

He swore to himself.

She was the one woman who had captured him and stolen his heart and soul. He'd never wanted her more.

She stopped in front of him and looked at

him over the rim of her glass as she took a sip of her wine.

He took her free hand in his. "You're late."

She pursed her lips. "I know. I had trouble getting into my dress."

Slowly, he let his gaze drop down the length of her. "It was worth the wait."

He pulled her a little closer, wrapping his arm around her bare shoulders. Her skin was as smooth as satin and warm to his touch. The soft floral scent of her drifted over him, causing his heart to accelerate.

He guided her toward their waiting guests.

"You look stunning, Reb," he whispered in her ear, feeling her shiver against his lips.

She smiled up at him. "Only for you, darling."

"There you are," Evelyn called.

In the next instant Rebecca was surrounded by numerous guests, leaving Gabe on the outside of the quickly formed circle.

Jonathan appeared at his side. "She's lovely."

Gabe gave his wineglass to a waiter as the music in the background picked up into a sultry love song. He shoved his hands into his pants' pockets. "I agree."

"You are a foolish man if you let her go," he said, never looking in Gabe's direction.

"I agree," Gabe repeated.

Jonathan smiled at him. "Then perhaps you wouldn't mind if I danced with her."

"Not at all. But not until I do." Gabe walked toward his wife.

It would only take a kiss, a whisper.

Just one night. That's all he wanted.

Then he could walk away, couldn't he?

EIGHT

A couple hours later, while the party was still in full swing, Rebecca and Gabe snuck away, returning to Evelyn's estate alone.

They silently strolled down the walkway toward the dark, quiet guest house. Reb had hoped they'd come back early, but now she felt as if her heart would burst, it was pounding so fast.

Gabe had his suit jacket slung over one shoulder, and his tie was loose at his neck, the top button of his tailored shirt undone.

"Say, what's this?" Gabe asked, stopping by the pool.

Rebecca drifted past him, dropping her beaded purse onto a chaise lounge. She pulled a chilled bottle of champagne out of the crystal wine cooler.

She skillfully popped the cork and poured the liquid into a glass.

"This is for you." She took a step closer until they were a breath apart.

Gabe traced a finger along her jawline to her lips.

He dropped his jacket over the back of the chair, then took the glass from her, allowing their fingers to touch.

"You captured every man's heart tonight."

She smiled. She'd been teasing and flirting with him, throwing her own emotions into a haywire mess the entire evening, hoping he'd notice.

"I only want yours." She dipped her finger into the chilled champagne and swirled it in a gentle circle.

"You've always had mine," he murmured. "That's never changed."

Raising her champagne-tipped finger to his lips, she ran her finger back and forth before slipping it into his mouth.

He closed his lips around her finger and twirled his tongue in a soft motion.

She couldn't stop the tiny gasp that escaped, as spirals of delight shot up and down her. She dipped her finger in the drink again and placed her fingertip into his waiting mouth.

"Are you teasing me?" He brushed a loose curl off her cheek with his knuckle.

She shivered. "Ah, no."

He lowered his head and touched his lips to the curve of her neck. "Are you sure?"

His warm breath fanned the soft skin under her ear.

She nodded. "Positive."

Gabe motioned to his side. "I'm not going to ask how all this got here, but what shall we do with the assortment of fruit?"

"Let's make it up as we go."

He smiled at her. "You're the adventurous one. Any suggestions?"

"I know a good way to start." She reached around and unzipped her dress, the sound of the zipper's metal teeth parting ringing softly in her ears.

With her hand, she swept a spaghetti strap off one arm and then the other until the sparkling concoction lay in a pool of sequins at her feet.

"What are you trying to do, Reb? Seduce me?" His voice was low and tempting, luring her closer. "Because it's working. Ever since I saw you swimming topless in this pool you've had me wound up in knots. There's no place for me to go."

Her pulse doubled.

"I won't ask you to make any promises you can't keep."

She stepped out of the dress and stood before him in black silk panties, lacy stockings and her high-heeled shoes.

She placed her palms on his broad shoulders and gently eased him into a sitting position on the chaise lounge. She moved closer, nudging one leg between his thighs. His arousal was clear to see. She propped her other leg on the cushion of the chair.

Slowly she unhooked the lacy edge of her stocking from the garter, and rolled it down an inch.

"Take it off, Gabe," she instructed huskily. "Undress me."

He swallowed hard. "Looks like you've already done that."

His words were as hot as she felt.

"Not completely," she purred.

He ran both palms up her silky leg, resting at the top of her thigh. She could feel the subtle strength of his fingers, the tenderness she knew he possessed. His touch on her sensitive flesh burned.

He leaned closer, lightly placing small kisses on the exposed inside portion of her thigh.

Rebecca let her head roll back, feeling the arc of electricity spark inside her with each brush of his fingertips, with each kiss.

"How's this?" His voice betrayed how aroused he was.

She pressed her fingers into his shoulder muscles, making him groan. "You're doing just fine."

He rolled the silk stocking down a couple of inches, stopping only to kiss and taste her trembling flesh. His tongue lightly traced a circular path, moving up, then down. "You taste as wonderful as you look." He slipped her sandal off, then the stocking.

"Gabe." She struggled for the words as she arched her hips toward him.

"Ah, darling," Gabe whispered, "you move me."

Lifting her other leg, he rolled the stocking down a couple of inches only to follow the same path with his tongue.

"That's the idea," she said in a shaky breath as her eyes fluttered shut. "I want to move mountains for you, Gabe."

After stepping out of her last shoe and stocking, she removed the silk tie around his neck and tossed it over his jacket.

There was a tingling in the pit of her stomach as she caught his fevered gaze. She unbuttoned each button of his shirt, pulling the fine cotton broadcloth from the waistband of his pants.

She ran her hands underneath the collar of his shirt, marveling at the smooth, hard flesh of his muscled back and his shoulders.

She smiled to herself when he trembled under her fingers as she removed his shirt, which landed on top of the tie and jacket.

"Reb."

"Yes, darling?" she murmured sweetly.

He drew her closer to him, so close the very core of her was just a warm breath away.

"You know we're not going to stop tonight." He rested his hands on her waist, squeezing gently.

"I know. That was the idea."

He gave a little chuckle. "Now that doesn't surprise me."

Fear surfaced in her. If he rejected her now, she didn't know what she would do. For a moment she couldn't talk. "Is it working? The seduction part, I mean?"

"Try and stop me." His voice was deeper

than normal, and the steamy air around them seemed to rise a few degrees.

She leaned over to the large platter of fruit on top of a table next to them, her breasts coming dangerously close to his face.

He growled low in his throat.

She selected a sliced orange and took a bite, letting a drop of juice drip down her bottom lip. Then she licked the juice away.

"I was hoping you'd say that."

"Just as long as you know that there is no turning back."

"I'm a big girl now."

"I know."

She placed the fruit to his lips and gently squeezed the rind, causing juice to trickle down his mouth.

She felt him tense as she moved closer. She licked the juice from his lips, letting her tongue linger over his lips, tasting the tangy fruit, tasting him.

He took the orange from her. "I can do better than that."

She arched her brows. "Then show me."

He started at the base of her throat where her pulse beat wildly, drawing the sweet, sticky fruit down her chest, giving a little squeeze when he circled her breasts.

Goose bumps sprang across her skin.

He pulled her to him, capturing one nipple between his lips. He rolled his tongue over the rosy, hard peak with tantalizing possessiveness. His tongue caressed one sensitive swollen nipple, then the other.

She moaned, aching with hunger and wild with desire.

His tongue was light and painfully teasing as he made a path down her taut stomach to the swell of her hips.

He squeezed the remaining juice over the black silk of her panties, soaking her until a trail of orange juice ran down her inner thigh.

Rebecca let out a small whimper.

He paused to kiss her stomach, licking away the sticky juice. He mumbled words she couldn't understand while his fingers hooked inside her silken panties, jerking her to him.

She arched her back.

His tongue, warm and moist, touched her through the thin fabric, causing her to suck in a sharp breath.

He kissed her again, and she could have

sworn he burned the black silk and lace clear off her body.

He moaned, drawing the lacy material down to her knees and off. "This isn't going to stop, Reb. I can't . . . stop."

"Don't stop. Please, Gabe, don't."

His tongue sank into her, licking and moving with light circular motions, sending jolts of pure ecstasy through her.

Gabe couldn't think about anything but Reb. He'd forgotten how incredible it was being with her like this, and every muscle in his body tightened with need for her. Never had he felt so alive.

Her eyes were shut, her neck arched, and her lips were parted and moist.

He could see the pulse at the base of her throat, beating wildly, making him ache for her even more.

With each caress her breathing became more erratic.

Watching her build to her climax was the most sensuous thing he'd ever experienced in his life.

He moved his mouth over her most sensitive flesh, making her tremble. He could feel his arousal burning hotter and hotter, straining for release.

He tasted the sweetness of the orange against her skin. He relished her. And she was the sweetest thing he'd ever tasted.

She shivered. She was so delicate, so feminine.

And his . . . for the moment.

"Ah, Gabe, I—" She stiffened, and a soft groan escaped her. Her eyes shot open, and their gazes met in a hot, feverish stare.

"Reb?"

His mouth throbbed.

And she throbbed, quivered and shook in one quick spasm against his mouth as her release took her.

"Oh, my . . . Gabe," she sobbed and laughed at the same time as her body went limp against him, the weight of her pressing them down on the chaise lounge. "I can't remember it ever being so . . . intense. What you do to me, I can't explain."

He took in her flushed face, the rosy dew across her chest. She was beautiful. And she was his. "I never underestimated you, Reb," he said on a ragged whisper.

"And I'll never underestimate you." She snuggled closer.

Naked chest pressed against naked chest.

She guided his hand to her. She arched her back, drawing him closer, inviting him.

He put one finger into her, and found she was moist, hot, filled with wanting him.

"Reb, sweet, Reb." He sucked in a deep breath. "So wonderful."

He kissed her lips, tasting faint traces of the orange that lingered on her tongue.

She groaned her surrender as he deepened the kiss.

He quickly moved his mouth from her lips to her ear while his hands explored the softer parts of her body.

The only thing he could hear was the pounding of his heart.

Warm night air hit his legs and lower portion of his body as he realized Reb had opened his pants.

With a quick movement, she pushed his pants down over his hips, to his knees, and then she dropped his pants to the ground. The rest of his clothing followed.

Shock registered then quickly disappeared as the tips of her breasts touched him once more.

She kissed his chest, nipping gently as the excruciating tension inside him built stronger and stronger until he thought he was going to explode.

He felt fear rise in his throat, mixed with the raw urge to be one with her.

All of a sudden he found it almost impossible to breathe, to move, and he knew that he was still in love with her. So much, in fact, that he would give her the child she wanted.

He willed himself to lift his head, to gaze at her.

Her hair, which at the beginning of the evening had been artfully piled on top of her head, now hung in riotous curls around her shoulders and face.

In one quick movement, he swung her underneath him. He grasped both of her hands in his, raised them over her head and held her there. He gently kneed her legs apart and settled between her.

He ran his tongue from her ear to the side of her temple, kissing her lightly, cherishing her more than words could ever express.

"Gabe."

Flames of sensation washed over him at the sound of her voice saying his name. Never before had the mere mention of his name affected him so deeply.

He looked at her and saw the loving invitation of wanting in her eyes.

"Now, Gabe. Please. I can't wait anymore." She offered herself to him, as she always had in the past. Nothing was held back. She was open and filled with love.

Longing welled inside him. He wanted her too.

He came to her, gliding into her tight warmth.

Tiny tremors rippled along his spine, burying deep inside his heart and soul.

She moaned. The sound between ecstasy and longing was heaven to his ears.

The soft moonlight caressed her face, and her slight smile was enough to make him tremble inside.

Soft strands of her hair brushed across his forearm as she moved. She grasped his thighs to pull him closer to her.

"Easy, love. It's been a long time for me. But I'd swear you feel like it's your first time."

"It is my first time with you again," she said in a breathless voice. "It's always been only you."

Gabe's heart soared. He kissed her lips, pushing a little deeper into her.

Their slow strokes became bolder, quicker, and they moved together as one soul, one heart, giving and taking with each movement.

"Gabe, I want more," she gasped.

"More?"

"Yes, please, don't stop."

"Baby, you're more than I could ever handle. I, ah, I don't think—"

"Just love me, Gabe." She crushed her lips to his, their tongues tasting, licking, sucking desperately with need.

With each thrust his concentration faltered. He was lost.

He clenched his teeth together, forcing his release to hold on for one minute longer.

One second longer.

Then he couldn't think anymore as the tremors of his release took over.

He grabbed her tightly in his arms, letting out a groan and feeling totally out of breath. He kissed the side of her temple, drawing the scent of her perfume deep inside his lungs.

She didn't say a word.

"Let me hold you for a moment," he said.

He shifted his weight off of her and drew her

close to his chest and into the safety of his warm embrace. He wanted to keep her if only for a few minutes, in a way that was his and his alone, no matter how wrong they were for each other.

As their breathing settled, he clung to her for a few moments longer.

She rolled over, angling her hips against him in the most provocative way.

If she kept this up, he thought, there'd be more than holding and touching.

There would be more memories to be made and to be cherished. Their lovemaking would lead to other passionate moments of making love, which would lead to other commitments and hopes of a reconciliation.

And more broken hearts.

He frowned as he felt the warmth of her skin, and the deep, regular breaths she took.

It was then that he noticed that she had drifted into a light, easy sleep.

He swore to himself. He felt like a bastard. Now what?

NINE

Rebecca's dream jarred her awake the next morning.

She opened her eyes. Gray peeked through the partially closed shutters, telling her that dawn was about an hour away.

The dream she'd been having wasn't particularly a good one, but it didn't matter. She knew Gabe was gone without even turning over.

Her chest tightened. The silence that ran through the small bedroom was almost deafening.

Slowly, she sat up, pulling the sheet to her chin. She stared, nearly hypnotized, at the far wall, feeling her insides crumble into a heap as she tried to ignore the hurt that pierced her heart. After all, what more could she do?

Gabe was gone. But that was what she had expected, even though she had hoped for the opposite.

She'd hoped she would wake up to him still lying beside her, that he'd make love to her all over again.

Gabe still hadn't let her inside his heart, she realized. His pulling away from her was proof enough. Their relationship was going nowhere.

With a heavy sigh she crawled out of bed, walked into the bathroom and turned on the shower.

One thing was certain, last night wouldn't happen again, she thought, looking at her rumpled appearance in the steamy mirror. She'd give him all the space he needed. Let him make all the moves.

She wasn't going to let him see how much he hurt her.

After all, turnabout was fair play.

Wasn't it?

"Gabriel Stewart, you haven't heard a word I've said." Evelyn stirred another spoonful of sugar into her tea.

"You've been in that stupid daze ever since you sat down this morning."

"I see you're in a good mood too," he commented dryly, thankful that he and Evelyn were the only ones left in the main house, the others having left early for a round of golf. He wasn't up to carrying on a civil conversation with anyone.

His head was pounding, and his stomach wouldn't stop churning. The promise he'd made to himself about keeping his distance from Reb had been all but destroyed in one incredible, passionate night.

A night he'd probably regret for the rest of his life.

Almost as much as he'd treasure its memory.

He stared at the mug of hot coffee he cradled in his hands, hands that had sweetly caressed his wife just a few short hours before.

"You look awful. Rough night?"

"Keep going, Evelyn," Gabe warned, hoping she'd drop the subject.

"Well you didn't stay long enough at the party to have a hangover," Evelyn continued, her sharp comments grating on his nerves.

Evelyn took a sip of her tea. "Besides, I know what you look like when you do have a hangover. And that's not what I'm seeing right now."

Evelyn leaned closer. "She turned you down, didn't she?"

Gabe shoved his coffee aside. "You know, Evelyn, one of these days I'm going to disown you."

Evelyn laughed. "Disown me? Hah, you've got that one turned around. I should disown you for being the stubborn jackass you are."

"You don't know when to quit, do you?"

"Oh, my dear boy. I can read you so clearly. You're stuck and don't know what to do. That beautiful granddaughter-in-law of mine has finally gotten the best of you, and you can't handle it."

She waved Hines to her side. "I'd like a mimosa." She challenged Gabe with her steely glare.

"Evelyn," Gabe warned.

"And don't lecture me about drinking this early in the day," she told him. "I think a celebration is in order and a mimosa sounds good."

Before Gabe could utter a smart retort, Rebecca walked into the garden room.

"Morning, everyone." Her voice was velvet-edged and husky.

Her body gently brushed against his shoulder

as she passed him, leaving behind a light scent of jasmine and freshly washed hair.

His gaze traveled up her tanned legs and the soft lavender bicycle pants she was wearing.

She poured herself a cup of coffee and stirred in a little cream.

He watched her every movement, her every breath as the memories of what it was like to be loved by her drifted through his mind.

His head pounded harder. Good Lord, he didn't need this.

Actually the truth was, he didn't want to get hurt. The fear that Reb would leave him again ate at his insides. He couldn't make her happy and though he wished it was just a sex thing between them, he knew in his heart it was much, much more.

He didn't want to think about it or the fact that more heartache was sure to follow if he didn't set the record straight.

Rebecca smiled as she sat next to him, giving him a better chance to watch her.

She appeared calm, rested and even a little bit cool. Perhaps a little too cool. Which wasn't what he was expecting.

"Sleep okay?" she asked. She took a leisurely sip from her mug.

She had her hair pulled up in a loose ponytail, a few unbound tendrils falling down the back of her neck.

His gaze wandered up her neck, to her ear, to her face and lips.

"Fine. How about you?" he asked, feeling his control slip a notch.

He waited for any sort of reaction on her part. A smile, a touch of her hand on his.

Anything.

She sat as still as a doll, staring contentedly into her mug of coffee.

The muscles in his forearm hardened beneath the sleeves of his royal-blue polo shirt. He wanted to touch the tender spot under her ear with his tongue and assail her with his kisses.

"I don't remember falling asleep." She leaned back in her chair as though she didn't want to sit so close to him.

"As a matter of fact, after the party, I don't remember a thing."

"It was a lovely party, wasn't it, Rebecca dear?" Evelyn asked.

"Oh, yes," Rebecca agreed.

Gabe could only stare at the two of them as they began discussing the evening before, completely ignoring him.

Reb's voice was calm, her gaze steady. She was acting as though the intimacy they'd shared the night before never had happened.

He should be happy that she was behaving this way. It sure would make walking away a lot easier. It was exactly what he had wanted. No ties, no commitments, no strings.

But for some strange reason he felt angry.

The night before had changed everything, had made him realize his true feelings for her.

When Evelyn finally left the garden room to make arrangements for breakfast, Gabe grabbed Rebecca's wrist.

"Just what the hell do you think you're doing?" he asked as calmly as he could.

She eased away from his grip and scooted back a bit, the amusement dying from her green eyes. "I'm trying to enjoy a cup of coffee."

He braced both of his hands on either side of her chair and pulled her over to him.

"You know what I'm talking about." He forced his hands to relax, and fought the urge to haul her onto his lap and smother her with deep, hard kisses.

She leaned close to him, her body not quite touching his. Her breath fanned his ear, sending hot desire straight through him. "I don't have a clue as to what you're talking about."

He hesitated, measuring her for a moment. "What happened between last night and this morning?"

"We had a nice time. That's all."

"Is that it?" He studied her face, searching for some sign of the emotion she'd shown the night before.

"Gabe, what do you want me to say?"

"I think last night was a mistake," he blurted.

"I'm sorry you feel that way." Her interest shifted from him to the coffee mug in front of her.

He swore under his breath. Everything was going wrong. Why couldn't he express his feelings?

"Reb, what if you're pregnant?"

She rested her hand on his arm. He loved the soft feel of her skin against his. It was difficult not to get distracted by just having her near him.

"I told you that you didn't have to get involved."

"But I am."

"You don't need to be."

Gabe went still. "You think I could walk away

if you're pregnant?" He felt as though his heart would stop beating any second.

"Yes, I do." Her voice was cool, but Gabe could see the doubt in her eyes. "We had an agreement. If I am pregnant, I'll deal with it on my own."

Gabe's stomach pitched. He was so confused, he couldn't even think straight.

"It's okay," she whispered. "Things will work out, I'm sure." She brushed her lips across his in a bittersweet kiss meant for lost lovers.

Before Gabe realized what he was doing, he pulled her off her chair and onto his lap.

She let out a gasp of surprise.

He wrapped her legs around his waist, and tried, though unsuccessfully, to ignore the heavy arousal between his legs as she settled on top of him.

He'd spent most of the last evening convincing himself he didn't still care for her, to no avail. Now he was convinced more than ever that he *was* in love with her and that scared him out of his mind.

He shoved his hands into her hair, molding his palms to her head. He pulled her closer to him until his mouth seared over hers in a hot, burning kiss—a kiss both punishing and angry.

But he didn't know if he was more angry with himself for letting his emotions get out of control or with Reb for making him feel in the first place. He ran his mouth up the side of her face to her ear, kissing wildly.

"Is that all you want?" he asked. "Just my child?"

"Gabe, ah, I—"

"What do you want?" he demanded again.

She let her head tilt back, and he bent his head to kiss the hollow of her throat where her pulse was beating wildly.

"Answer me." His rough voice betrayed his impatience and annoyance. He gazed at her, waiting for her reply.

She moaned softly and started to pull away. Her eyes were glazed, and her lips were pink and moist. She took a slow, deep breath.

He brushed back the loose curls that had fallen out of her ponytail. The smooth skin along her neck was red from his kisses.

For a second he was convinced she still wanted him as much as he wanted her. He thought he could see it in her eyes, in the way she responded to him.

Then she slowly eased off his lap and returned to her own chair.

He suddenly felt cold and alone.

"I've come to the conclusion that you've been right all along."

"About what?" he asked, feeling his emotions strain to their limits.

"We're not right for each other. We don't love each other."

Her words stung.

"And so, I don't want anything more from you," she said, "except for you to fulfill your promise to help me set up my day care center. I have my license already and with Jonathan's donation I'm sure I'll be able to pull it off."

She didn't mention the other part of their bargain, and he didn't know what to say.

"I'll keep my word about the business." He swallowed. "You don't have to worry about that."

She gave him a weak smile just as Evelyn walked back into the room.

"Good. Then, there's nothing left to discuss," Rebecca said. "Let's have breakfast."

TEN

It had been a couple of days since he and Rebecca had their rather tense encounter in the garden room when she'd told him the biggest lie of her life.

In his heart he knew she loved him, almost as much as he loved her. He could tell by looking into her eyes.

And with each passing day it was getting more difficult to concentrate on the business at hand—if the mounting paperwork on his desk was any indication—and he hadn't heard a word Jonathan had said to him all morning.

"I think that takes care of all the details to date." Jonathan gathered up the papers in front of him.

"What? Oh, yes, Jonathan," Gabe said, feeling as though he'd just had a bucket of cold water thrown in his face. "I'll have our proposal ready by the end of the day so you can look over the final offer."

Jonathan chuckled as he watched him. "Do you still feel that thrill of closing a deal?"

"Ah, what, Jonathan?"

Jonathan leaned back into the leather chair as though measuring his words. "You know, I see you making the same mistakes I've made."

"Excuse me?"

"When I was younger," Jonathan said, "my mind was always on business. Nothing else. Almost ruined my marriage and my family.

"I'd oversee this or restructure that," Jonathan continued, his voice taking on a softer tone than Gabe had ever heard him use. "I always had my fingers in the day-to-day running of the business, whether it was going to battle over some managerial decision or the fun parts that came with owning my own company. I was always at my best during a crisis. It always gave me a real thrill, a high. Do you understand what I mean?"

Gabe nodded. The truth was the thrill was gone. And had been long before the negotiations had started on this merger. The only difference was now he had finally admitted it to himself.

Jonathan put his papers in his briefcase and walked to the library door. "This merger is important. I don't want you to think otherwise. But I do hope you can recognize when the excitement isn't there anymore and that you do something about it before it's too late."

Gabe looked up at the older man at that moment, realizing the truth in his words.

And he knew why the thrill of high stakes and balancing a multimillion-dollar corporation had died for him.

Reb.

Plain and simple. She'd captured his heart and soul.

"I hope you're right, Jonathan." Gabe silently thanked the older man for some good fatherly advice.

"I suppose I'll see you later this evening for our last formal dinner together with the board members. Oliver and I will be leaving for London first thing tomorrow."

Gabe walked to the door and shook Jonathan's hand. "Whatever the outcome on this merger, I want you to know, Jonathan, it's been a pleasure."

"Thank you." Jonathan gave Gabe a smile before leaving.

Rebecca walked down the hallway from Evelyn's bedroom suite with an armful of clothing and a notebook in her free hand. She didn't see Gabe until she ran smack into his chest.

"This is a pleasant surprise."

She felt herself blush. It was silly, of course, that he could still get to her. That just being near him made her skin tingle and her heart do flip-flops.

She stared at him. "If you're looking for Evelyn, she just left for her hair appointment."

"I'm not."

"I had to remind her about her appointment for the third time." Rebecca tried to calm her erratic pulse. "I'm sure she'll be late."

Gabe rubbed his knuckles across her cheek, sending a wave of heat to soar through her. "You're always thinking of others, aren't you, Reb?"

She shrugged, looking at the beige carpet. "I don't think about it. It just comes naturally."

"Naturally sweet, you mean."

She glanced at him, knowing she couldn't have loved him more.

"You've been avoiding me," he said.

"I suppose I have. I've had a lot to do helping Evelyn get ready for the dinner party tonight and all." She indicated the armful of clothing she held. "I promised Evelyn I'd iron her dress."

"I remember how you used to do those same things for me. I never told you how much I appreciated it, did I? I suppose it's too late now."

"It's never too late to tell someone how you feel, Gabe. Maybe if you had, things would have been different between us. I don't know."

She shrugged, trying to throw off the bittersweet feelings he was evoking in her.

"I'm leaving tomorrow," she said, finally.

He tipped her chin up with a lift of his finger. "I know."

It was just as well, she concluded. The sooner she returned to her normal routine, the easier it would be to get a sense of order in her life.

She waited for what seemed like an eternity, but he didn't say anything else. She didn't know what she expected him to say.

Maybe that he wanted her to stay?

Maybe that he loved her?

"Well I better be going or we'll all be late for the party," she said, and continued walking down the hall.

Rebecca sighed and followed the others into the banquet room at the Indian Springs Country Club where Evelyn had put together an intimate farewell dinner party for all her guests.

"Here, let me get your chair for you." Jonathan stood behind her seat as everyone sat down.

"Thank you." She sat down, feeling herself blush.

She glanced across the wide table, catching Gabe's stare. His expression was closed and unreadable as if he was in deep thought. At that moment she would have given anything to know exactly what those thoughts were.

"I dare say, Rebecca"—Jonathan pulled his seat up next to hers—"you look extraordinary tonight."

"Thank you, Jonathan." She ran her hand down the flare of her short gold metallic dress.

"Giving you compliments is certainly an easy thing to do," Jonathan said. "You've been by far the loveliest of company on what has turned out to be a rather tedious mission."

Rebecca accepted the glass of champagne the waiter poured for her. "I hope your *mission* was successful."

Jonathan raised his glass and clinked it against hers. "Very. I won't be seeing you before I go. But rest assured I will certainly continue to help with your day care center."

Rebecca smiled again, knowing he was sincere.

"I'll miss you, Jonathan. And I truly thank you for all your help. I hope that when the merger is complete, we'll have another chance to meet."

"I suppose that will depend on your husband."

Some sixth sense brought her attention across the table of china, silverware, and crystal stemware to meet Gabe's dark, penetrating gaze.

Gabe raised his champagne glass to her and then took a sip.

Yes, she thought, feeling her stomach tighten. It all depended on her husband.

"I suppose you're right, Jonathan." She dragged her gaze away from Gabe.

"Would you care to dance?" Jonathan asked.

Rebecca shot one last glance at Gabe, longing for the protectiveness of his warm embrace.

"Of course, Jonathan. That would be lovely."

Gabe silently observed his wife across the room as she danced gracefully in Jonathan's arms.

The wily old man had managed to monopolize all of Reb's attention throughout dinner, dessert, and finally the last dance of the evening.

Gabe watched Jonathan turn Rebecca. The glittery flare of Reb's gold dress flipped the other way, exposing a shimmering, silky leg to his view.

He took a deep breath and tried to ease the knots of tension in his neck.

Ever since the morning after they'd made love, Reb had maintained her cool demeanor and her distance.

The sweet smiles were gone, as well as every luscious bit of attention she'd heaped on him in the last two weeks.

Never to return.

Gabe had never felt more alone in his whole life.

You can't have it both ways, he sighed to himself. You can't have Reb and divorce her too.

He looked across the dance floor when the song ended. He couldn't tear his gaze from Reb as Jonathan walked her to the table.

Rebecca picked up her purse, and a fire stirred in Gabe's body as he watched her lithe movements. He wanted to get her attention, let her know he still cared for her, something.

A smile, a look, anything.

"If you'll excuse me for a moment." Before he even had a chance to speak, she was gone.

Jonathan straightened his tie and sat down. He picked up his champagne glass, and motioned for Gabe to sit down.

"You know, Gabe," Jonathan said after a few seconds, "you remind me of myself when I was a young man."

Gabe sighed. "So you've told me."

Jonathan raised his glass in Gabe's direction. "Except that I'm honest and you're not."

Gabe shot straight up in his chair. "Jonathan, I beg your pardon. I have never once been dishonest with you. The dealings with The Toy Factory are above reproach, and my grandmother and I—"

Jonathan laughed. "Please calm down. I'm not talking about your business dealings or this merger."

"What do you mean?"

"I mean you are not honest with yourself. Or Rebecca."

"Jonathan, I don't think—"

"Let me finish. I know about your divorce. I

know Rebecca is only here to put on a show for me."

Gabe felt the color drain from his face. His stomach started to churn as he saw his entire future vanish.

Jonathan straightened his tie as though he realized he'd said too much. "Excuse my bluntness, but I'm a man who speaks his mind. A woman like Rebecca is one in a million."

Gabe could only nod, he was so stunned.

"Perhaps it is none of my business what you do in your personal life, but I'd never let a woman like her out of my grasp."

Gabe knew exactly what Jonathan meant.

Jonathan stood as Rebecca returned to the table.

Gabe caught her gaze.

She gave him a smile.

The warm smile he'd been waiting for all night.

A hundred emotions sprang inside him. Yearning, need, hope.

He wanted to touch her, wanted to remove the pearl studded pins that held her hair up on top of her head.

He wanted to bring each silky strand to him and breathe in the clean scent.

She was an aphrodisiac to his senses, and he could feel his heartbeat vibrating with pure energy.

He wanted her heart more than anything else.

And what he wanted right then was to dance with her, hold her in his arms. He knew the band was about to leave, but he'd just have to change that, he thought reaching deep in his pant's pocket for his wallet.

Hell, he'd paid for the band and if it cost him triple the fee to have the last dance with his wife, then it would be worth the price.

She was his lady, and she simply took his breath away.

She'd gone into hiding, and he wanted her back.

Rebecca went still at the touch of Gabe's hand on her shoulder.

"I want to dance with you," he whispered in her ear, sending shivers up her back.

She closed her eyes, feeling the warmth of his breath fanning the back of her neck, feeling the strength of him standing so close to her.

"The last dance."

Her heart pounded.

"I want to hold you in my arms, Reb. Feel you close to my heart."

"Gabe, ah, I—"

"We have one last night together. Don't take it away from me . . . from you," he added.

Gently and without any words, he took her by the elbow, and she let him guide her to the empty dance floor just as the musicians tuned up for the last song of the evening.

He took control in one easy motion, wrapping his strong arm around her waist, drawing her up against him.

She took in the woodsy scent of his cologne, the smoothness of his clean-shaven cheek as he lowered his face next to hers.

"You feel so good in my arms." His words were barely a whisper. "I love holding you like this, as if we're one."

"I know."

The song, a soft romantic lullaby, played across the dimmed banquet room, making her feel lost and loved at the same time, as he expertly moved her across the floor.

"I want to be alone with you," he said after a few moments.

She looked up at him, wondering if he could

hear the crazy pounding of her heart, wondering if he could see the love in her eyes. "Gabe, tell me what you're talking about."

The song ended on a low but sweet note, the sound sending shivers up her arms.

"I want to spend the night with you."

"But I thought you had said that . . ."

They stopped their movements, and he touched her lips with the tip of his finger. "We have this one moment to share. Let me, please."

Her breathing was becoming more and more erratic, her pulse beating wildly at her throat.

"Wait for me, my dear sweet Rebecca." He ran his finger along her bottom lip. "Promise me, you'll wait."

All she could do was nod.

Later that evening, Rebecca had showered and dressed in her new cotton knit pajamas. She sat down on the bed anxiously fingering the satin trim of the rose-print top.

She didn't know if Gabe had been serious when he'd told her to wait for him.

She thought about the pajamas she was wearing and how she'd bought them on a whim to tease him. She'd wanted to see his reaction when he saw her dressed in the conservative loose top and long-legged bottoms.

Though she never had the chance . . . until now.

What was keeping him? she thought. Their last night was slipping away.

She sighed and tossed the parenting magazine she'd been reading into the small trash can that was across the room.

"That was a lucky shot," Gabe said from the doorway of the bedroom. "Bet you can't do it again."

Rebecca looked up and felt her heart jump a beat.

"Care to make that bet?" she asked. "Put your money down."

"I think I better not." He walked into the bedroom. "I only like to bet when I know I'm going to win."

He was still dressed as he'd been at the dinner party except for his jacket. His tie was loose and his blue shirtsleeves were rolled up to his elbows.

He'd never looked more handsome.

She scooted across the mattress, making room for him on the cozy bed.

He sat down and rested against the headboard.

She watched him.

He smiled warmly at her.

Her breath caught, and she felt the heat flush up to her cheeks.

All of a sudden the air turned sultry.

"I wasn't sure if you'd come or not," she confessed.

"I had a couple of farewell drinks at the house. Everyone is leaving tomorrow."

"I know." She willed her emotions to stay calm.

"This last week, these last few days, actually, I've been thinking that maybe it's time for me to slow down, take it easy. I think that I've been working too hard."

"I've thought that many times too." She paused for a second. "Evelyn told me about the boarding schools your father sent you to."

Gabe took her hand in his. "I've thought a lot about that just this past week," he said. "It's funny how you think something is long forgotten from your past but really it isn't."

Rebecca nodded. "Maybe we have more in common than you thought."

He looked at her.

"Did you resent your parents for sending you away?"

He shrugged. "A little, I suppose." He gave a humorless laugh. "Hell, my mother, Ellen, split before that. I don't remember much about her. She hasn't been a part of my life since my parents divorced." The anger was clear in his voice.

Rebecca let him continue.

"I guess my father couldn't handle it. That's probably why I was sent away. He hid himself in his work."

The last few quietly spoken words trailed out of his mouth as though he realized what he was saying.

"Just like you."

He acknowledged her with a slight nod.

"I understand, Gabe. Really, I do."

"I know. And believe it or not, Reb, I think you were right."

She wanted to cherish the last quiet hours alone. She didn't want to think about tomorrow. And she didn't want to dwell on the past. It was all too painful.

"I'm glad." She stared into his eyes, wishing he'd kiss her, wishing for so much more.

"I'm glad you waited," he murmured.

He reached over and rubbed the satin trim of her pajamas. His warm fingers brushed underneath the cotton fabric, bringing a rush of pleasure to her already-heated skin.

"What in the world are you wearing?"

"Pajamas." Her breath caught as his fingers traced the curve of her neck.

"That's quite a switch for you. From satin and silk to cotton."

Slowly, he ran his finger back down her neck, stopping at her cleavage. He eyed the rose-print top, and then unfastened the top button with ease.

"You like?" she asked, feeling her temperature rise a few degrees.

He smiled. "Yeah, I like."

His finger stroked the soft skin between her breasts, sending shivers up and down her arms.

He removed his tie and tossed it to a nearby chair. Reaching for her, he drew her into his embrace, sighing loudly. "I'm tired." He pressed his lips to her temple in a light kiss.

She felt his lips curve into a smile as though some private thought amused him. "What's so funny?"

"Only that this last week and a half has been crazy. I'm not sure I'd ever want to go through that again."

She pulled away from his embrace and stared

at him. "We wouldn't have seen each other otherwise."

For a moment his eyes darkened with emotion. "You're right. And that would have been the worst thing that's ever happened to us."

"Gabe," she whispered. "What do you want from me?"

He seemed sure of himself as he took charge with quiet assurance. "Come here."

ELEVEN

In one magical heartbeat, she was by his side.

"I'm here," she murmured softly. "I've always been here for you."

Gabe wrapped his arms around Rebecca.

Touching her was a necessity.

Loving her was inevitable.

"Even though we can't be together, in my heart and mind, I'll always be with you." Her words struck him deep inside.

It was the same for him. When this was over and she was gone from his life, he knew she'd be in his thoughts, feelings. Even in his dreams.

He ran his hand down the long curve of her back, feeling the soft cotton of her pajamas and the inviting curves he knew lay beneath.

He undid another button on her pajama top,

watching her lids ease shut. She looked so peaceful, so happy, and he wished he could keep her that way forever.

"Hmmm?" she whispered.

"Reb, look at me."

Slowly, she opened her eyes, her gaze soft and full of promise.

"You love me, don't you, Reb?"

She froze for a few seconds. "You . . . you know I do, but it doesn't change that I'm leaving tomorrow."

"I know," he said. "But you're here with me tonight, aren't you?"

"I wouldn't have it any other way."

Gabe's chest tightened at her soft words of confession. God help him, but he loved her.

"Reb, let's play a game."

His gaze traveled from her lips to her wide eyes. Her hair, still piled up on top of her head, was artfully held together by those damn pearl studs.

Lord, but she was beautiful.

She gave him a smile. "What kind of a game?" Her voice trembled a little.

"I'm going to start touching you."

A surprised gasp caught at the back of her

throat as he removed one pearl stud, his finger lingering at the back of her neck.

A thick strand of hair fell, brushing against his hand. Her hair felt silky soft and cool on his skin.

"And you have to tell me what to do or I'll stop."

He brought the curls to him, inhaling deeply, just like he'd imagined hours ago. The scent, so fresh, so sweet touched him deep inside.

She wriggled out of his embrace to study him. "You're kidding."

He shook his head. "I'll stop unless you tell me what to do. Those are the rules. Okay?"

"Anything?"

He could see the skepticism in her eyes, hear the hesitation in her voice.

"Anything."

"What if I tell you to leave?"

"I'll have to leave."

He stroked her cheek with his knuckles, then with the back of his hand. He brought his fingers close to her mouth and watched as her lips parted on a sigh.

"But I have the feeling you're not going to tell me to leave." He drew little circles over her top lip, then her bottom lip. "Or rather, I'm hoping that you want me to stay."

She took in a sharp breath.

He could see that he was rousing her passion, as his own grew stronger. He was shocked at his eager response to touching her in this simple way.

"You're right," she said. "I'm not going to tell you to leave."

"So, you understand all the rules."

She nodded.

"All right." His voice was deceptively calm. "Tell me what to do."

She hesitated as though measuring each thought and action in her mind.

He waited, his heart pounding in his chest.

"I want to feel my hair hitting my shoulders. Look into my eyes and undo my hair."

Their gazes locked as they breathed in unison. He pulled a pearl-studded hairpin free. Then another. Then the last one.

Her hair cascaded across her shoulders and tumbled down her back in one shimmering mass.

A rush of pink stained her cheeks. "Run your fingers through my hair."

With both palms, he cupped her cheeks and ran his hands up her face and into her thick hair.

A quiver raced through his veins at the touch of her velvety curls.

She bit her lip to stifle her cry as he gently massaged her head and her temples.

She tugged on his arms, snuggling closer. "Hold me tight, Gabe. I want to feel your arms around me like you'll never let me go."

He brought a quick breath deeply into his lungs as though he was starving for air. It took a split second for him to wrap her in his arms.

"Closer," she whispered.

He choked back the moan and brought her roughly to his chest. The need for her cut through him like a knife, making him unsure if he'd be able to finish the game. The urge to make her his immediately was almost uncontrollable.

He wanted to give her everything, anything, even another chance at giving her a child.

A slight smile curved his lips. The change in him felt good. Even the thought of children felt good.

She pulled them down to the sheets, and buried her face against his throat. A few seconds later she gazed up at him. "What's wrong?"

"Nothing. You stopped, so I stopped."

She gave a small laugh and her eyes gleamed

with a white heat he hadn't seen before. "You're serious, aren't you?"

He lowered his head close to her ear. "Uh-huh," he whispered.

She shivered at his nearness. "Okay, I'll try. Rub my back."

He ran his large hand up her back and gently kneaded.

"No, under my top," she instructed in a soft voice.

Holding back a sigh of relief, he drew her to him. His hand slid under the floral pajama top with ease. He held his breath as he caressed the smoothness of her back, gently squeezing as he went. His fingers massaged deeply into her tight shoulder muscles, causing her to softly moan his name.

"That feels wonderful."

"You're doing good, Reb," he said, captivated by the feel of her under his exploring hands. "You catch on quick."

Reb closed her eyes and concentrated on the moment. Every nerve ending was alive. Every one of her senses and emotions was working overtime.

"Gabe?"

"Hmmm?"

"Unbutton my top."

A second later, Rebecca felt the last remaining buttons fall open. A wave of air hit her chest, cooling her heated neck, arms, and breasts. She looked at him. His eyes blazed so fiercely, she thought she'd never felt so aroused.

"Touch my breasts." Her voice nearly cracked with desire. Her breasts felt heavy, hot, in her anticipation of his loving caress.

His hand lightly touched her hardening nipples, drawing tiny circles around the hard nubs, then her entire breast.

"Kiss me now."

"Where?"

"Kiss my ear," she said, trying to control the shivers that shook her body. "I want to feel your tongue in my ear."

His lips were warm as he touched the soft spot below her earlobe. As he moved upward, his tongue traced the outer rim of her ear, then slowly explored the inside. He drew her earlobe into his mouth, making her squirm with delight.

His kiss was slow and thoughtful. Tender and spine-chilling.

"Kiss my neck. Don't forget my neck," she

urged. She wasn't about to let him stop the fever he was slowly creating inside her.

His lips seared a path down her neck, her shoulders, then quickly returned to the hollow at the base of her throat. Her pulse beat hard. Then in one swift movement his lips captured hers. His mouth was hard and demanding, sending new spirals of ecstasy through her, pushing every ounce of air from her lungs.

He pulled away for a second. "I'm sorry. I got carried away. I'm breaking my own rules."

She gasped for air. "I, ah, I was going to tell you to do that anyway. You move too fast for me, that's all."

He brushed his mouth across hers. "Then tell me, sweetheart. What do you want?"

"Kiss the back of my neck. My shoulders."

He pulled her to a sitting position, his mouth finding its way to the back of her neck. His kiss was urgent and exploratory in his need to satisfy her.

"Ah, yes," she moaned as he gently nipped at the back of her neck and in between her shoulders.

"How about my breasts?"

She fell back against the plump pillows.

"Gladly." He leaned over her, his lips teasing a taut, dusky pink nipple. Then the other.

"Touch me."

His hands, warm and smooth, slid up her firm stomach to the swell of her hips to her breasts. His caresses were light and painfully teasing.

"Squeeze them," she said, not being able to stand it anymore. "Kiss them again."

With both hands he cupped her breasts, running his thumbs over each nipple. Squeezing ever so gently, he brought her to him. His mouth closed over one nipple, licking and tasting her.

"Ooh, that feels so good."

"It feels good to me too." His ragged voice betrayed his mounting passion.

"Hold me tight," she commanded.

"Like this?" His hands moved gently down the length of her back, wrapping her closer to him.

"Yes," she sighed. Instinctively, her body arched toward him. His body imprisoned hers in a web of growing arousal.

"Gabe."

"What? Tell me what to do."

"Take off your clothes."

He eased away. With quick dexterity he unbuttoned his shirt.

She concentrated on the sounds of his irregular breathing and the pounding of her heart. She sunk lower into the softness of the bed, pushing aside the pillows.

She could hear the swoosh of his shirt as he yanked it off his arms, the cool sound of his zipper, the rustle of sheets, and the dropping of his clothing to the floor.

She swallowed the lump at the back of her throat. "Don't forget me." Their gazes locked in a heated stare.

He slid the pajama bottoms off her hips, down her legs. Discarding her bottoms, and the unbuttoned top, she lay naked beneath his gaze.

"Come here, and kiss my stomach."

The expert touch of his warm mouth on her heated skin sent her even higher. She cried out for release, grasping his head in her hands, holding him to her.

"Do you like this?" His lips brushed against her stomach as he spoke.

"You'll never know how much."

"How's this?" He kissed a little lower, then raked his tongue to the apex of her thighs.

"Oh, yes," she moaned. "Kiss my thigh."

He grabbed the warm flesh of her inner thigh and then he kissed her. Up and down.

Rebecca could only close her eyes and feel the hot, pulsating coil of her need near the breaking point.

His arousal was hard and ready.

"You're so good," she barely whispered. "Kiss me right there." She guided him closer.

"You're teasing me, Reb." He stroked her with his words.

Shivers vibrated through her body. "No, you're the one who's teasing. Don't stop. Please, don't stop."

"Close enough for you, sweetheart," he murmured softly against the softness of her skin.

"Almost," she softly cried.

She wanted to tell him to whisper words of love to her, but she couldn't.

She wouldn't.

"I want to make you purr," he murmured against her.

"I need to feel you." She stretched, as every muscle in her body ached and burned. "I want to feel you warm and hard inside me."

Exploding in a downpour of fiery sensations, she met him halfway as they joined together as one.

Maybe for the last time.

Waves of ecstasy throbbed through her.

She clutched his shoulders, and he buried his face in her neck, murmuring words she couldn't understand. She couldn't control the cry of pure delight and rapture as her body screamed for release.

Suddenly, he grabbed her hips and lifted her up against the headboard of the bed. When he pressed harder into her, she wrapped her legs around his waist and let her head drop close to his face.

She could feel the hardness of him pressing into her, throbbing as they rocked together in one passionate movement after another. She took in his scent, his breath, the burning heat that came from his body.

It was painful. It was heaven.

He pressed his lips into her neck. "Reb, we're almost there. Look at me."

Their gazes locked as the shuddering release shook them both over and over again.

He grabbed her shoulders, and with tangled legs and hot, slick bodies they slid to the mattress.

"Let me hold you," he whispered. "You feel so good in my arms."

He pulled up the floral sheet to cover them, the cotton cooling her heated body. He wrapped his arms around her, drawing her close to his chest.

"You'll always be mine, sweetheart," he murmured against the pulse of her neck. "Always."

She choked down the hot tears that came to her eyes. Her chest squeezed tightly as she listened to his heavy breathing ease to a slow, steady pace.

He'd never uttered a word about a reconciliation. Or that he loved her.

She only hoped that she had the strength to walk away because it would kill her more to stay.

TWELVE

"You're a damn fool," Evelyn said the second Gabe walked into the living room of the main house the next morning.

He took a deep breath and slumped onto the couch. "I suppose I am." If ever there was a time he had to admit that his grandmother was right, it was now.

He was a damn fool. Maybe even worse.

"She's gone, you know."

"I know." He'd known when he'd opened his eyes that morning. The small bedroom, where they had shared their last incredible moments together, had felt empty.

And he knew exactly why.

Reb was gone, and gone for good this time.

He took in another painful breath, telling

himself that it was best to end it this way. He should be happy that Reb had made it so easy for him by leaving the cottage while he was still asleep.

Yet he wasn't happy.

Far from it in fact.

"She left you this." Evelyn handed him an envelope. "She didn't want to see you, did she?" Evelyn sat next to him, giving him the once-over. "Can't say I blame her. You look awful."

He shrugged. Awful was putting it mildly. He felt tired and drained. He hadn't shaved or even bothered to put on clean clothes from the previous night.

"You're always ready with the compliments when I need them the most," he said dryly. "Thanks for the support."

"I've always been supportive, Gabe. But when I see you making an ass of yourself for the second time—"

"Evelyn, please, I don't feel much like arguing with you this morning."

Besides there was nothing she could say to him that he didn't already know.

He ripped open the envelope. A slim gold band slipped onto his palm.

Reb's wedding ring.

His throat constricted.

"She's . . . really gone." He placed the ring on the tip of his finger, holding the ring up in the morning light.

It was a sharp reminder of what he once had . . . and now didn't.

"Yes." Evelyn tapped his chest. "She's really gone and if you love her as much as I know you do, I'd say it's time you made some changes."

She smiled tenderly. "And I have some thoughts on the matter too, young man. That is, of course, if you're interested in hearing them."

He swallowed hard, knowing in his heart he was definitely ready for a major change. Knowing, too, that he'd do anything to get Reb back.

If it wasn't too late.

"I'm listening," he said.

Rebecca threw her outdoor gear and clothing into the back of the pickup truck. She had a few hours until her clients were to arrive at the Canyonlands National State Park where she, Linda and Jim Murphy were taking the crew of rafters down the Green River to the Colorado River.

It was Rebecca's last trip. Afterwards, she'd be opening her day care center in Phoenix.

Leaning against the closed door of the pickup, she scanned the buttes and mesas that loomed across the Utah horizon. Cottonwoods and willows lined the riverbank, their branches artfully arching over the water.

She breathed a huge sigh.

Lord, how she missed him. She missed him every second of every day. And even though it'd been two weeks since she'd left Palm Springs, it wasn't any easier to get him out of her mind.

Or her heart.

Even though she knew she had to.

She pushed the pain away, struggling to get her mind back on business.

Mentally, she went over her list of supplies for the trip.

She'd packed everything, or hoped she had anyway. Fishing gear. Tools. Boat repair kit. Flares. Food. First-aid kit. Too bad there wasn't a first-aid kit big enough to repair her broken heart.

"Hey, Rebecca." Jim came out of the state park office building. "We've got one last-minute sign-up. Some guy. Said it was real important he got on this trip."

Rebecca shaded her eyes from the hot sun.

"Great. Just great. I love these last-minute tourists."

"Yeah, well, he was real adamant about joining up. Said he needed a vacation."

"Probably some Wall Street shark who gets himself all tied up in knots and expects us to undo him." Rebecca felt frustration creep into her.

"It's all part of the business," Jim said. "I've got a few more things to get together and then I promised to pick up Linda." He patted Rebecca's shoulder. "It's good to have you back, even if it's only for this last trip."

"Thanks, Jim. It's good to be back."

She watched Jim leave, grateful for his and Linda's friendship, then returned her gaze to the supplies.

"You know, Rebecca," Gabe said softly from behind her. "You're the only one I'd ever let undo me."

Rebecca went completely still.

She slowly willed herself to breathe. She looked up and took in the sight of him.

He was dressed in rugged jeans, hiking boots, and a black T-shirt that brought out the devil-may-care look in his dark eyes.

He dropped his gear to the ground.

Where was his tie? she wondered, and his tailored suit and expensive shoes? Where was his cellular phone, and his endless list of business matters that had to be taken care of yesterday?

Never had he looked so handsome, so rugged and appealing, she thought as she fought back the memories of curling in his warm embrace, touching her lips to his.

She swallowed hard. "What are you doing here?"

He took a step closer, and the clean scent of him engulfed her with other memories she didn't want to remember.

"I wanted to surprise you."

She smiled and shrugged. "Well, it worked."

"I decided that I needed some time off from The Toy Factory."

"You're our last-minute sign-up?" She couldn't help but stare at him.

"Uh-huh. And I'm not even some Wall Street shark."

A hot flush crept up her cheeks.

"I told you I was going to start slowing down. Besides, we never had a chance to discuss the details about my donation."

"I see."

"Did you forget?" he asked softly.

"No, I didn't forget." She looked away.

He moved closer until they were inches apart, forcing her to look up at him. He towered over her, his gaze taking in every single feature as though he was burning them in his memory.

"There are a lot of things about you that I've forgotten. And that's not good." He ran his finger along her jawline, her chin. He touched the corner of her mouth.

Her lips tingled at his touch. But the tender gesture still had her pulling away.

"Maybe you never knew what you had in the first place," she said, wanting to hurt him as much as he'd hurt her.

He smiled a little. But it was a sad smile. "Well put, Reb. And true."

"So why are you here?"

"I wanted you to know that I've changed. I realized that all my life I've been so worried about getting ahead, and taking care of my family that I never took the time to learn what was really important. I used my career as a defense against getting too close, caring too much. Working was the only aspect of my life that I could truly control. It was the only thing I understood. Only it backfired. I don't want to wind up alone and bitter like my father."

She stared at him for a moment. "So what are you saying?"

"I'm here to tell you that I want you back." His voice, so calm before, quivered.

"I don't believe you," she whispered.

He gently placed his hands on her shoulders, and drew her to him. His lips came down on hers in a slow, tender kiss.

It was as though he was pleading with her to surrender to him, as his kiss turned urgent.

She swayed under his gentle persuasion. And had it not been for his arms tightly wrapped around her, she surely would have collapsed.

It was the most exquisite kiss he'd ever given her.

"I want you to believe me." His lips brushed against hers as he spoke. "I don't want anything but you."

She refused to let her tears fall. She swallowed with difficulty and found her voice. "Gabe—"

"I wanted to see you again because I need you, because I love you . . . because I want to marry you."

Gabe couldn't let her go. Not until he convinced her how he felt.

He'd lied when he told her they didn't have a future together, that they were incompatible. He'd been afraid to believe in what they had. But everyone saw how perfect they were together. Jonathan, Evelyn, even Reb.

And now he realized it too, and he was determined to try to make things right between them.

He took a deep breath.

"I made the biggest mistake of my life. Not once, but twice," he confessed. "And that was letting you go."

She jerked away, but not fast enough.

"Gabe, please don't do this to me . . ."

"I can't help it." He caught her again in his arms. "I love you. So much that it scares me. But the thought of losing you again scares me even more. Don't leave me, Reb." His voice broke. "Don't ever leave me."

"How do I know I can trust you?"

"Because I've changed," he said. "I know what's important now and what isn't."

He smiled again. Softer this time. "And you've changed too," he added. "Or rather I finally met the real Rebecca Stewart in Palm

Springs. You're not just the wild, fun-loving free spirit I thought I married."

She smiled back. "Well, who am I?"

"You're my wife."

"Ex-wife," she said. "Or did something happen a week ago to stop our divorce that I don't know about?"

"No, the divorce was final last Tuesday. But in my heart, you will always be my wife. You're caring and giving. You always think of others first, which is why I fell in love with you a second time."

"I . . ."

"I know I'm rushing you." He rubbed his hands up and down her arms. He couldn't stop touching her.

"What about us not being compatible?"

He searched her face. "I was wrong. I thought there wasn't a future for us. I thought I wasn't ready for children. But now . . . now I want children. Lots of them."

He saw her swallow. "I don't know what to say."

He brushed aside an escaping curl that fell over her forehead. "Tell me you love me. Tell me that you need me as much as I need you."

"Gabe," she whispered. "Gabe, I've always loved you. I never stopped loving you."

He placed his lips to her neck. Her skin tasted dusty and hot.

"What about my day care center?"

"You can open a center anywhere," he said. "Last I heard there's plenty of kids who need looking after . . . even in Palm Springs. And I happen to know there's an empty building next to The Toy Factory. There's lots of space and open areas for a playground. More room than you'd ever need. I happen to know the owner."

"Who?"

"Me," he said. "And it could be an added bonus for the employees to have the day care center next to the office."

"Gabe, that sounds wonderful, but—"

"Don't you deserve to be happy?"

A tear glinted in the corner of her eye. She wiped it aside with the back of her hand. "Yes."

"Don't I?"

"Of course."

He gestured with his hands. "So why are you fighting with me about this?"

"I . . . what about The Toy Factory?" she asked.

"I've made a decision to step down as CEO.

I'm passing the magic scepter to Jonathan. I'm on a leave of absence right now."

"You didn't."

He smiled at her. "Yeah, I did. Evelyn and I agreed completely. I have enough money to last a lifetime. And I want to spend my life with you."

He reached into his jeans' pocket and withdrew her wedding band. He slipped it on her finger.

"Damn, Reb, I thought I died a thousand times over when I saw this in that envelope."

He squeezed her hand in his.

"I felt like a part of me died too, when I left it," she said.

"Ah, sweetheart." He slowly kissed her, vowing to spend the rest of his life erasing the pain from her eyes. "So, do you have any other arguments?" he asked. "Or will you marry me?"

"No more arguments. And yes, I'll marry you."

He laughed out loud. He picked up his rolled-up sleeping bag and swung it over his shoulder.

"Okay, let's go then."

Before she could answer, he picked her up in his arms, and headed for the thick grove of cottonwoods that lined the river.

She let out a shriek of surprise. "Where are you taking me?"

"Do you think you could find us a quiet, secluded area to hide out for an hour or two?" he asked.

Rebecca started to laugh. "Oh, I suppose I could. But what for?"

He stopped and let her slide down the front of him until her feet touched the ground.

"Because I'd like to be alone with my future wife for a while." He playfully kissed the corners of her mouth. "You see, I know this game I'd like to play. And I just found my perfect partner."

LOOK WHAT THE STORK BROUGHT!!!

NAMES: Meg and Chip
DATE: May 1, 1996
WEIGHT: Meg—8 megabytes
Chip—6 microchips
PARENTS: PINK and Einstein

Special thanks to:

1st place—Carol Quinto for the name Meg A. Byte
1st place—Anne O. Ryan for the name Chip
2nd place—Carolyn Maxey for the name SKAMP (Super Kid Adored by Mega Prototypes)

Many thanks to all who entered the "Name the Computer Baby" Contest. Turn the page for profiles of our first place winners!

Carol Quinto lives in Deltona, Florida, with her husband, Mike, and two psychotic cats. Carol and her husband have been married for twenty years, and are still very much in love. An avid reader and true romantic at heart, Carol particularly likes contemporary romances (Loveswepts, naturally), Patricia Potter historicals, regencies, and mysteries. Fortunately, she shares the same tastes with her mother (who lives next door), so they are able to trade books. Both Carol and her mom are devoted fans of Einstein and PINK, and are thrilled about their new additions!

Anne O. Ryan and her husband of twenty-six years live in DeFuniak Springs, Florida, where they are the proud parents of seven children and four grandsons. Anne is an elementary school teacher, a volunteer for the PTA, Cub Scouts, Boy Scouts, and Little League Soccer, the secretary of the North Walton County Republican Club, and a member of her local Methodist church. Anne also loves to sew, crochet, and travel. And did we mention that Anne loves to read? Well, she does, voraciously, sometimes devouring as many as twenty books a week!

THE EDITORS' CORNER

Next month come celebrate LOVESWEPT's THIRTEENTH ANNIVERSARY with a stellar lineup of your favorite authors, who prove that spooky thirteen, even the more chilling Friday the Thirteenth, can bring the best kind of luck. In each of their novels, the hero and heroine experience unexpected twists and exhilarating turns in their lives—and before they know it, they're swept away into the most passionate journey of all. So put your superstitions aside and join us next month on an exploration of the romantic power of thirteen.

Victoria Leigh casts an irresistible spell in **WAIT FOR MIDNIGHT**, LOVESWEPT #790. He usually draws people to him the way a magnet beckons steel, but attorney Ben Philips has never ached to charm a lady into his life as he does when he spies Kate Hendricks in her hospital flower shop. Stunned by unexpected yearning, Kate meets temptation with a tease—until she discovers Ben's ruthless interest in a mysterious patient she's taken under her wing. Victoria Leigh delivers tenderness and sizzle for a top-notch romantic read.

Praised by *Romantic Times* as "fascinating," the MAC'S ANGELS series by award-winner Sandra Chastain continues with **SINNER AND SAINT,** LOVESWEPT #791. Nikolai Sandor doesn't want to feel anything for the sleeping woman who resembles a fairy-tale princess, but only he can give Karen Miller a reason to live! Murmuring endearments, he tries to convince her they are more than strangers . . . until she awakens and begs her gypsy lover to make her fantasies come true. But can she forgive him for not promising forever? If you're looking for enchantment, then Sandra Chastain's beguiling novel is perfect for you.

Thrilling romance and breathtaking suspense ignite the pages of **PLAYING WITH FIRE,** LOVESWEPT #792, by Debra Dixon. Haunted by a long-ago secret hidden deeper than a dream, Maggie St. John can't brush aside the finger of suspicion arson investigator Beau Grayson points her way. He senses she knows more about the hospital blaze than she's telling him, and he's determined to get the truth—even if it means challenging her to face her tragic past. Summer is about to get hotter with this scorching novel from terrific talent Debra Dixon.

Mary Kay McComas is at her delightful best in **GOT IT BAD,** LOVESWEPT #793. When Dr. Mack McKissack storms the fortress of Kurt Andropov's laboratory to discover what he might be concealing, she doesn't plan on staying any longer than she has to in the devil's lair! Then a shocking accident places her in isolation with the maverick genius, and Mack has to deal not only with the unknown bug that threatens their lives, but also with the fiery attraction arcing between two rivals on the edge. Mary Kay McComas delivers pure gold with this hilarious, outrageous, and heartwarming romance.

Happy reading!

With warmest wishes,

Beth de Guzman	Shauna Summers
Senior Editor	Editor

P.S. Watch for these Bantam women's fiction titles coming in June: From Jane Feather—the incomparable author of national bestsellers VIOLET and VALENTINE—comes **VICE,** her newest unforgettable romance. Suzanne Robinson takes readers back to the Victorian world of LADY DANGEROUS in **THE ENGAGEMENT,** a mesmerizing love story about a freethinking young woman and a gun-toting Texan. Bestselling author Sandra Canfield, author of DARK JOURNEY, presents a gripping tale as a desperate call from the past throws a man and a woman together again in **NIGHT MOVES.** Finally, from Susan Johnson, the award-winning mistress of sizzling historical romance, comes **SWEET LOVE, SURVIVE,** the powerful conclusion to the bestselling Kuzan Dynasty series begun in SEIZED BY LOVE and LOVE STORM.

Be sure to see next month's LOVESWEPTs for a preview of these exceptional novels. And immediately following this page, preview the Bantam women's fiction titles on sale now!

Don't miss these extraordinary books by your favorite Bantam authors

On sale in April:

THE UGLY DUCKLING
by Iris Johansen

THE UNLIKELY ANGEL
by Betina Krahn

DANGEROUS TO HOLD
by Elizabeth Thornton

THE REBEL AND THE REDCOAT
by Karyn Monk

NEW YORK TIMES BESTSELLING AUTHOR

IRIS JOHANSEN

MAKES HER SPECTACULAR HARDCOVER DEBUT WITH A THRILLING TALE OF ROMANTIC SUSPENSE

From her award-winning first novel to her latest triumphant success, Iris Johansen has been heralded as a dazzling storyteller of incomparable brilliance. Now she reveals a new side to her talent, weaving an exciting tale of contemporary suspense that gives the age-old myth of transformation a stunningly unique twist . . . as an ugly duckling becomes a breathtaking beauty whose burning wish for revenge entangles her in a precarious world of sinister intrigue and desperate desire. . . .

THE UGLY DUCKLING

Plain, soft-spoken Nell Calder isn't the type of woman to inspire envy, lust—or murderous passions. Until one night when the unimaginable happens . . . and Nell's life, her dreams, her future are shattered by a spray of bullets and the razor edge of a blade. Though badly hurt, Nell emerges from the nightmare a woman transformed, with an exquisitely beautiful face and a strong, lithe body. While Nicholas Tanek, a mysterious stranger who compels both fear and fascination, gives her a reason to go on living. But divulging the identity of her assailant to Nell might just be the biggest mistake of Tanek's life. For he will find his carefully laid plans jeopardized by Nell's daring to strike out on her own. And Nell will find her mission imperiled by Tanek's dangerous magnetism, a temptation to which she cannot afford to surrender.

"Crackling suspense and triumphant romance with a brilliant roller coaster of a plot."

—Julie Garwood

"Only Iris Johansen can so magically mix a love story with hair-raising adventure and suspense. Don't miss this page-turner."

—Catherine Coulter

"A fascinating, compelling drama with myriad strands of intrigue swirling around a heroine who will let nothing stop her in her quest for vengeance." —Linda Howard

"A fabulous, tension-packed romantic suspense novel with seething emotions and deadly secrets that lure the readers into a fascinating web of intricate design." —Kay Hooper

"You look like a princess." Jill rocked back and forth in her bed, hugging her knees.

"Not likely." Nell gently pushed her down on the pillows and pulled up the blanket. "Now don't try to stay awake. Take a nap and I'll wake you when I bring our picnic. One of the maids will be right outside in the sitting room." She teasingly ruffled her daughter's hair. "Just in case you see any monsters."

"I did see him, Mama," Jill said gravely.

"Well, you won't see him again." She kissed her forehead. "I promise you."

She had reached the doorway when Jill called, "Remember the wine."

Nell chuckled as she shut the bedroom door. Jill would never suffer from either shyness or inability to assert herself.

Her smile vanished as she passed the mirror in the hall. Only her daughter would see anything princess-like in her appearance. She was almost five eight but definitely plump rather than Junoesque. Plump and boring and plain as grass. Her features were nondescript except for a nose that turned up instead of fading into the boring sameness as the rest of her face. Even her short brown hair was boring, the same pale acorn shade of Jill's without childhood's sheen. Plain.

Well, Jill thought she was beautiful and that was enough for her. Not that Richard didn't think she was attractive. He had once told her she reminded him of a country quilt, enduring, traditional and beautiful in its simplicity. She wrinkled her nose ruefully at her reflection before moving quickly toward the door. She didn't know one woman in the world who wouldn't rather be a glamorous silk sheet than a country quilt. But plain women had one advantage; no one ever noticed when they entered or left a room. She would have no trouble escaping the ballroom with Jill's picnic supper.

She stood at the top of the marble stairs looking down at the crowded foyer.

Music.

The scent of flowers and expensive perfume.

Laughter and conversation.

Dear God, she didn't want to go down there. The tall carved doors leading to the ballroom were thrown wide open and she could see Richard standing in a corner talking to a tall bearded man with a ribboned chest. Kavinski? Probably. Martin, Sally and Nadine were also crowded around him and Sally's expression was almost fawning. Nell would be expected to meet Kavinski later but she would only be in the way now.

Her gaze searched the room and she finally spotted Madam Gueray in the shadow of the french doors. Elise Gueray was fiftyish, thin and trying desperately to blend into the white velvet drapes. Nell felt a swift rush of sympathy. She knew that frozen smile and hunted expression; she had seen it in her own mirror.

She started down the stairs. Let Richard charm Kavinski and wheel and deal with everyone else in sight. Helping Richard by making that poor woman less miserable was much more to her taste.

"*Mon dieu*, the man should have a rose in his teeth," Elise Gueray murmured.

"What?" Nell put a lemon tart on the tray. She had promised Jill a chocolate eclair but she couldn't see any on the buffet table.

"You know, like Monsieur Schwarzenegger in that movie where he played the spy who could do everything except fly?"

She vaguely remembered the movie and the huge Schwarzenegger tangoing with a rose in his teeth. "True Lies?"

Elise shrugged. "I never remember titles but Schwarzenegger is hard to forget." She nodded at someone across the room. "And so is he. Do you know who he is?"

Nell glanced over her shoulder. The man Elise was indicating did not have Schwarzenegger's height or bulk but she could see what Elise meant. Dark haired, middle thirties, with a face more arresting than good looking, he exuded total self confidence. He would never be caught in a situation he could not control. No wonder Elise found him fascinating. For people like her and Nell such assurance was as appealing as it was unattainable. "I've never seen him before. Perhaps he's in Kavinski's entourage."

Elise shook her head.

She was right, Nell realized. This stranger would not travel in anyone's wake.

"Are you that hungry?" Elise's gaze had shifted to Nell's tray.

Heat scorched her cheeks. "No, I thought I'd take a selection up to my daughter."

Elise looked stricken. "I did not mean—"

"I know." Nell made a face. "I don't exactly look underfed."

"You look very nice," Elise said gently. "I did not mean to hurt you."

"You didn't." She grinned. "It's my predilection for chocolate cake that hurts me. It's as comforting as a security blanket."

"And do you need comforting, my dear?"

"Don't we all?" she evaded, then said more firmly, "No, of course not. I have everything I could possibly want." She added softly, "If you have time, I'd like you to meet my daughter tomorrow."

"I would enjoy that very much."

"Oh, there are the eclairs. She loves eclairs." She added the pastry to the treasures on the tray before turning back to Elise. "Will you excuse me? I'd like to take these up to Jill. I told her to take a nap but she's probably still awake."

"Certainly. I've taken too much of your time. You've been very kind."

"Nonsense. I've enjoyed it. I should be the one to thank you." It was the truth. Once her shyness was dispersed Elise Gueray revealed herself to possess both humor and wit. She had made the last few hours pass pleasantly enough. Nell picked up the tray. "If I don't see you later this evening, I'll call you after breakfast tomorrow."

Elise nodded, her gaze going to her husband across the room. "I doubt if I'll be here when you return. Henri will be ready to leave soon. He only thought it important he meet Kavinski."

Nell edged around the crowd, her brow creased in a frown of concentration as she balanced the heavy tray.

The wine.

She stopped short outside the ballroom doors.

Oh, why not? A few sips wouldn't hurt Jill, Europeans fed it to their babies all the time. She wanted Jill to be happy tonight. Who knew how many more opportunities they'd get to just be together.

She ducked back inside the ballroom. Champagne. Even better. As she grabbed a glass of champagne from a passing waiter, the tray she was balancing in her other hand wobbled.

The tray was taken from her. "May I help you?"

Arnold Schwarzenegger. No, at closer range he resembled no one but himself. Very high impact. That confidence was overpowering and she instinctively wanted to escape it. She pulled her gaze away from his. "No, thank you."

She tried to take the tray but he held it out of her reach. "I insist. It's no trouble." He strolled out of the ballroom and she was forced to hurry after him. "Where is this assignation to take place?"

"Assignation?"

He glanced down at the tray. "He must have a hearty appetite."

She felt the heat sting her cheeks. Twenty-eight years old and she was blushing. She muttered, "It's a treat for my daughter."

He smiled. "Then I assume the assignation is still to take place in a bedroom and you'll never make it up the steps with the champagne *and* the tray." He moved across the foyer and started up the staircase. "I'm Nicholas Tanek and you are . . . ?

"Nell Calder." She found herself running after him. "But I don't need help. If you'll give me—"

"Calder? Richard Calder's wife?"

He was surprised. They were always surprised Richard had chosen her. "Yes."

"Well, he appears too busy to help you. Permit me to substitute."

He was clearly not going to be dissuaded. She might as well let him have his way. It would be the quickest way to rid herself of him. She followed him up the steps and found herself watching the smooth flexing of his shoulders and buttocks. Both were sleekly muscled and extremely admirable.

"How old is your daughter?"

Her gaze guiltily flew upward but he was still looking straight ahead, she realized with relief. "Jill's almost five. Do you have children, Mr. Tanek?"

He shook his head. "Which way?"

"Right."

He asked, "Are you with Continental Trust too?"

"No."

"What do you do?"

"Nothing. I mean—I take care of my daughter." When he didn't comment she found herself continuing on. "I have quite a few social duties."

"I'm sure you're very busy."

But not like the women in his world. She was sure they were all sleek and gifted and as confident as him.

"You're American?"

She nodded. "I was raised in Raleigh, North Carolina."

"That's a university town, isn't it?"

"Yes, my parents taught at Greenbriar University just outside Raleigh. My father was president of the college."

"It sounds like a very . . . secure life."

He meant boring. She bristled. "I enjoy small towns."

He glanced back over his shoulder. "But, of course, it can't compare to the life you lead now. I'm told Continental Trust's European headquarters is in Paris."

"Yes, it is."

"And it must be pleasant being able to visit places like this. Luxuries can be very important."

"Can they?"

"I was speaking to your husband earlier in the evening. I'd judge permanent life in a palace would suit him very well indeed."

"He works hard to earn any luxuries we enjoy." His idle probing was beginning to annoy her. He could not really be interested in either Richard or her. She changed the subject. "Are you in banking, Mr. Tanek?"

"No, I'm retired."

She stared at him, puzzled. "Really? You're very young."

He chuckled. "I had enough money and decided not to wait for a retirement party and a gold watch. I now own a ranch in Idaho."

He had surprised her again. She would never have thought he was the type to wander far from the urban life. "You don't seem—"

"I like the solitude. I grew up in Hong Kong surrounded by people. When I was in a position to choose, I opted for wilderness."

"I'm sorry, it's none of my business."

"No problem. I have nothing to hide."

She would wager he had a great deal to hide, she thought suddenly. He was a man who buried everything beneath that smooth surface. "From what business did you retire?"

"I dealt in commodities." He asked, "Which door?"

"Oh, the last one on the left."

He moved swiftly down the corridor and stopped before the suite.

"Thank you. It wasn't necessary but I—"

He had opened the door and was striding in, she realized in astonishment.

The Greek maid hurriedly sat upright in the chair.

"That will be all," Nicholas Tanek said in Greek. "We'll call you when we need you."

The maid walked out of the suite and closed the door.

Nell stared at him, stunned.

Tanek smiled. "Don't be alarmed. My intentions are above reproach." He winked. "Well, unless you call avoiding a very boring party reproachful. I saw you bolting out the door and I needed an excuse to get away for awhile."

"Mama, did you bring—" Jill stood in the doorway, her gaze on Tanek. "Who are you?"

He bowed. "Nicholas Tanek. You're Jill?"

She nodded warily.

"Then this is for you." He presented the tray with a flourish. "Mead and ambrosia."

"I wanted eclairs."

"I believe we have those too." He swept toward her. "Where will we dine?"

Jill studied him for a moment and then capitulated. "Mama and I are going to have a picnic. I put a blanket on the floor."

"Excellent idea. You're obviously ahead of us." He started setting the paper plates down on the blanket. He said over his shoulder, "You forgot the napkins. We'll have to improvise." He disappeared into the bathroom and returned a minute later with a pile of tissues and two embroidered hand towels. "May I, madam?" He draped the hand towel around Jill's neck and tied it in the back.

Jill giggled.

Nell felt a ripple of resentment as she saw that Jill was enjoying the novelty of attention from a stranger. This was supposed to be her time together with her daughter and he was spoiling everything.

"Thank you for helping me with the tray, Mr. Tanek," she said formally. "I know you want to get back to the party."

"Do I?" He turned to her and the smile faded from his lips as he searched her face. He nodded slowly. "Yes, perhaps I should return." He bowed to Jill. "But I'll wait to take back your tray, madam."

"Don't bother," Nell said. "The maid can get it in the morning."

"I insist. I'll wait in the sitting room. Call me when you're ready." He strode out of the bedroom.

"Who is he?" Jill whispered, her gaze on the half open door.

"Just a guest." She was surprised that Tanek had given up so easily. Well, he had not given up entirely. It was clear he didn't want to return downstairs and was using the suite as a haven. Who was he avoiding? A woman, probably. He was the kind of man who would have women chasing him. Well, she didn't care as long as he stayed out of the way and didn't bother them.

"I like him," Jill said.

Nell didn't doubt it. Tanek had made sure Jill felt like an empress in those short minutes.

Then her eyes fastened eagerly on the crystal goblet, and she instantly forgot about Tanek. "Wine?"

"Champagne." Nell dropped to the floor and crossed her legs. "As you commanded."

Jill's radiant smile lit her face. "You brought it."

"It's a party." She handed her the glass. "One sip."

Jill took a huge swallow and then made a face. "Sour. But it's kind of warm and bubbly going down." She lifted the glass again. "Jean Marc says that—"

Nell snatched the glass from her. "Enough."

"Okay." Jill reached for the eclair. "But if it's a party, we should have music."

"Right." Nell crawled over to the nightstand, reached for the music box and wound it. She set it down on the blanket and they watched the two panda bears spinning slowly on the lid. "Much better than the orchestra downstairs."

Jill inched closer, lifted Nell's arm and fitted herself beneath it. As she munched on the eclair, pastry flakes fell on Nell's blue lace gown and Nell knew that before Jill was through chocolate icing would be all over both of them.

She didn't care. To hell with the gown. Her arm tightened around her daughter's small warm body. Moments like this were rare and precious.

And might become even rarer.

No, she couldn't let them do it. Richard was wrong and she must convince him that Jill needed her.

But what if she couldn't convince him?

Then she would have to fight him. She felt panic and despair rise at the thought. Richard always made her feel as if she were being both unreasonable and cruel when she disagreed with him. He was so certain of everything and she wasn't sure of anything.

Except that it was wrong to make her give up her daughter to a faceless stranger.

"You're squeezing me too tight," Jill said.

She loosened her hold but kept Jill close. "Sorry."

"S'okay." Her mouth full of pastry, she rubbed against Nell forgivingly. "Didn't hurt."

She had no choice. She would find the strength somewhere. She must fight Richard.

He had come here for nothing, Nicholas thought in disgust as he gazed down at the surf crashing on the rocks below. No one would want to kill Nell Calder. She was no more likely to be connected with Gardeaux than that big eyed elf she was now lavishing with French pastry and adoration.

If there was a target here, it was probably Kavinski. As head of an emerging Russian state he had the power to be either a cash cow or extremely troublesome to Gardeaux. Nell Calder wouldn't be considered troublesome to anyone. He had known the answers to all the questions he had asked her but he had wanted to see her reactions. He had been watching her all evening and it was clear she was a nice, shy woman, totally out of her depth even with those fairly innocuous sharks downstairs. He couldn't imagine her having enough influence to warrant bribery and she would never have been able to deal one on one with Gardeaux.

Unless she was more than she appeared. Possibly. She seemed as meek as a lamb but she'd had the guts to toss him out of her daughter's room.

Everyone fought back if the battle was important enough. And it was important for Nell Calder not to share her daughter with him.

No, the list must mean something else. When he went back downstairs he would stay close to Kavinski.

"Here we go up, up, up
High in the sky so blue.
Here we go down, down, down
Brushing the rose so red."

She was singing to the kid. He had always liked lullabies. There was a reassuring continuity about them that had been missing in his own life. Since the dawn of man mothers had sung to their children and they would probably still be singing to them a thousand years from now.

The song ended with a low chuckle and a murmur he couldn't hear.

She came out of the bedroom and closed the door a few minutes later. She was flushed and glowing with an expression as soft as melted butter.

"I've never heard that lullaby before," he said.

She looked startled, as if she'd forgotten he was still there. "It's very old. My grandmother used to sing it to me."

"Is your daughter asleep?"

"No, but she will be soon. I started the music box for her again. By the time it finishes, she usually nods off."

"She's a beautiful child."

"Yes." A luminous smile turned her plain face radiant once more. "Yes, she is."

He stared at her, intrigued. He found he wanted to keep that smile on her face. "And bright?"

"Sometimes too bright. Her imagination can be troublesome. But she's always reasonable and you can talk to—" She broke off and her eagerness faded. "But this can't interest you. I forgot the tray. I'll go back for it."

"Don't bother. You'll disturb Jill. The maid can pick it up in the morning."

She gave him a level glance. "That's what I told you."

He smiled. "But then I didn't want to listen. Now it makes perfect sense to me."

"Because it's what you want to do."

"Exactly."

"I have to go back too. I haven't met Kavinski yet." She moved toward the door.

"Wait. I think you'll want to remove that chocolate from your gown first."

"Damn." She frowned as she looked down at the stain on the skirt. "I forgot." She turned toward the bathroom and said dryly, "Go on. I assure you I don't need your help with this problem."

He hesitated.

She glanced at him pointedly over her shoulder.

He had no excuse for staying, not that that small fact would have deterred him.

But he also had no reason. He had lived by his wits too long not to trust his instincts and this woman wasn't a target of any sort. He should be watching Kavinski.

He turned toward the door. "I'll tell the maid you're ready for her to come back."

"Thank you, that's very kind of you," she said automatically as she disappeared into the bathroom.

Good manners obviously instilled from childhood. Loyalty. Gentleness. A nice woman whose world was centered on that sweet kid. He had definitely drawn a blank.

The maid wasn't waiting in the hallway. He'd have to send up one of the servants from downstairs.

He moved quickly through the corridors and started down the staircase.

Shots.

Coming from the ballroom.

Christ.

He tore down the stairs.

Explosions.

Firecrackers, Nell thought absently. Sally had told her there would be a fireworks display to crown the evening. She must have stayed upstairs longer than she had thought. Sally would not be pleased.

The stain wasn't too bad. Thank God for the miracle of carbonated water. She had been afraid she would have to change. She dabbed carefully at the chocolate smear.

She heard a door shut in the sitting room.

The maid. What was her name? Hera. "I'm in the bathroom. I'll be leaving in a moment, Hera. I managed to smudge my—" She looked up.

A face in the mirror, pale, shimmering, distorted.

"What—"

The glimmer of steel, an arm lifting.

A knife.

She whirled as the knife descended.

Pain.

The knife was wrenched from her shoulder and plunged down again.

He must be a thief. "No—jewels. Please."

The dagger entered her again, this time carving her upper arm. She could see the attacker's lips drawn back from his teeth, through the stocking mask. Not a thief. He was enjoying this, she realized in horror. He was toying with her. He liked to see her pain and helplessness.

The blood was running down her arm and the pain was so intense it was making her sick.

Why was he doing this?

She was going to die.

Jill.

Jill was in the next room. If she died, she couldn't keep him from hurting Jill.

He was raising the knife again.

She kneed him in the groin.

He grunted in agony and doubled over.

She pushed past him. He felt strange, rubbery against her body. She staggered into the sitting room. Her knees were shaking. She was going to fall.

"Bitch." He was right behind her.

She had to have a weapon. No weapons.

She yanked out the cord of the lamp on the table beside her. She threw the lamp at him.

He deflected it with one arm. He kept coming.

She backed away from him. Didn't they tell you your best defense was to scream?

She screamed.

"Go ahead. No one will hear you. No one will help you."

He was right. The firecrackers and cries from downstairs were too loud.

She was standing by the french doors that led to the balcony. She tore down the beige silk drapes and tossed it over his head. She heard him cursing as she darted past him.

Almost past him.

He freed himself in time to grab her arm and jerk her to her knees. He raised the knife again.

She lunged upward, her head striking him in the stomach.

His grasp loosened and she wrenched free.

"Mama."

Oh God, Jill was standing in the doorway of the bedroom.

"Stay away, baby."

The balcony. If she could lure him out onto the balcony, Jill might be able to escape.

Her fist lashed out and connected with his cheek. She whirled and ran out onto the balcony.

He followed her.

"Run, Jill. Go to Daddy."

Jill was crying. She wanted to comfort her. "Run, bab—" The knife. Stabbing. Pain.

Fight him.

Weak.

Strike out. Hurt him.

Give Jill time to get away.

Run.

No place to run.

The balustrade stone hard and cold against her spine.

Make him fall. Make him fall over the balcony. Her arms clutched desperately at his shoulders as she tried to turn him.

"Oh, no, you stupid whore." He broke free and shoved her over the balustrade.

She was screaming.

Falling.

Dying.

Nicholas fought his way through the panicked guests pouring out of the ballroom into the foyer.

He grabbed Sally Brenden's arm as she ran past. "What happened?"

"Let me go." Her eyes were glittering with terror. "Crazy. They killed them. Crazy."

His hand tightened on her arm. "Who fired the shots?"

"How should I know?" She turned to a heavy set man who had emerged from the ballroom. "Martin!"

Martin Brenden was pale and sweating.

"Kavinski's down. And two others. And I saw Richard fall. They shot Richard."

"How many are they?" Nicholas asked. "Where are the shots coming from?"

"Outside, through the window," Martin said. "Kavinski's body guards are after them." He grabbed his wife's arm. "Let's get out of here."

"How could this happen?" Sally asked dazedly. "My wonderful party . . ."

"They'll be found." Martin patted her arm. "Kavinski had two men posted at the dock. They'll never get away from the island."

She let him lead her away. "My party . . ."

Nicholas pushed through the crowd to the front door.

Two men running, their bodies lean and darkly gleaming in the moonlight. Wet suits.

They weren't heading for the docks but toward the far end of the island.

Of course, not the docks. Gardeaux would have found a way to avoid that trap after the targets were hit.

Target.

Nell Calder.

He whirled and ran back into the palace.

She was too good to be true.
He was too bad to resist.

Experience the enchanting wit of
New York Times bestselling

BETINA KRAHN

author of *The Last Bachelor* and
The Perfect Mistress

in the delicious new love story

THE UNLIKELY ANGEL

With her soft heart and angelic face, Madeline Duncan is no one's idea of a hardheaded businesswoman. So when the lovely spinster comes into an unexpected inheritance and uses her newfound wealth to start a business, she causes quite a stir . . . especially with barrister Lord Cole Mandeville, who has been appointed by the courts to keep Madeline from frittering away her fortune. Handsome, worldly, and arrogant, Cole knows just how ruthless the world can be—and that an innocent like Miss Duncan is heading straight for heartbreak, bankruptcy, or worse. But when he sets out to show Madeline the error of her ways, Cole is in for the surprise of his life . . . as he finds himself falling under the spell of a woman who won't believe the worst about anyone—even a jaded rogue like him.

"One of the genre's most creative writers. Her ingenious romances always entertain and leave the readers with a warm glow."
—*Romantic Times*

Spellbinding. Intoxicating. Riveting.
Elizabeth Thornton's gift for romance is nothing less than addictive. Now from this bestselling author comes her most passionate love story yet.

DANGEROUS TO HOLD

by

ELIZABETH THORNTON

He'd accosted her on a dark London street, sure that she was his missing wife. But a few moments in her company assured Marcus Lytton that Miss Catherine Courtnay was nothing like Catalina. Cool and remote, with a tongue as tart as a lemon and eyes that could flash with temper, the fiery-haired beauty was everything his scheming adventuress wife wasn't—innocent, loyal, and honest. And so he uttered the words that would sweep Catherine into his life, and into a desperate plan that could spell disaster for them both: "I want you to play the part of my wife. . . ."

"You are, are you not, my lord, a *married* man?"

The smile was erased. "What do you know of my wife?" he asked.

She hesitated, shrugged, and said boldly, "Until tonight, I knew only what everyone else knows, that you'd married a Spanish girl when you served with Wellington in Spain."

"And after tonight?"

This time she did not falter. "I know that you hate her enough to kill her."

His eyes burned into hers, then the look was gone and the careless smile was in place. "You have misread the situation. It is my wife who wishes to kill me. She may yet succeed. Oh, don't look so stricken. I believe it happens in the best of families. Divorce is so hard to come by, and for a Catholic girl the word doesn't exist." His voice turned hard. "So you see, Catalina and I are bound together until death us do part. An intolerable situation."

Her mind was racing off in every direction. There were a million questions she wanted to ask, but she dared not voice a single one. Even now he was suspicious of her. She could feel it in her bones.

She tried to look amused. "I'm sure, my lord, you are exaggerating."

"Am I? I wonder." His mood changed abruptly. "Enough about me. I am at a disadvantage here. I know nothing about you, and until I know more, I refuse to let you go."

He spoke gaily, as though it were all a great game, but she wasn't taken in by it. She'd seen that darker side of him and knew that the danger wasn't over yet. She intended, if at all possible, to leave this place without his knowing who she was or where to find her.

She moistened her lips. "My lord, I appeal to you as a gentleman to let me go. You see, there is someone waiting for me. If he were to hear of my . . . misadventure, it could prove awkward for me."

There was a strange undercurrent in the silence, as though her words disturbed him in some way. "I see," he said. "And this gentleman, I take it, is someone you met tonight at Mrs. Spencer's house. Did you make a secret assignation?"

Alarm coursed through her veins. "Mrs. Spencer? I know no one by that name."

"Don't you? I could have sworn that I saw you leave her house tonight. What happened? Did you quarrel? Did she throw you out in those rags? I know how jealous women can be. And you are very beautiful. Did you steal one of her lovcrs? Is that it? Who is waiting for you? Is it Worcester? Berkeley? Whatever they offered, I can do better."

A moment before, she had been trembling in her shoes. Now a wave of rage flooded through her. Each question was more insulting than the last, and he was doing it on purpose. This time, when she rose to her feet, there was no tremor in her knees. She was Catherine Courtnay and no man spoke to her in those terms. "My business with Mrs. Spencer," she said, "is no concern of yours."

"So, you were there!"

"And if I was?"

There was a moment when she knew she had made that blunder she had tried so hard to avoid. He rose to face her and his eyes glittered brilliantly. Then he reached for her, and hard, muscular arms wrapped around her, dragging her against thighs of iron and a rock-hard chest. She could feel the brass buttons of his coat digging into her. Her arms were trapped at her sides. One hand cupped her neck, then his lips were against her mouth.

From the exciting new voice of

KARYN MONK

author of *Surrender to a Stranger*

THE REBEL AND THE REDCOAT

"Karyn Monk . . . brings the romance of the era to readers with her spellbinding storytelling talents. This is a new author to watch." —*Romantic Times*

When he saw the lovely young woman struggling with her captor, Damien didn't care which side of the bloody war she was on. He only knew that he had never seen such extraordinary beauty and raw courage in his life. Yet Damien couldn't know that one day this innocent farm girl was destined to betray him. She would become Charles Town's most irresistible spy, dazzling officers with her charms even as she stripped them of strategic secrets. But when a twist of fate brings Josephine back into his life again, Damien will gamble everything on the chance that he can make this exquisite rebel surrender . . . if only in his arms.

Jo stiffened with terror as she lay on the ground and waited for the Indian's blade to carve into her back. Despite her determination not to show her fear, a sob escaped her lips. She was going to die. She waited for her body to be ruthlessly stabbed. The Indian fell heavily onto her, crushing her with his weight, and she screamed, a scream born of utter despair. She had failed. Now Anne and Lucy and Samuel would die. The warrior jerked a few times. Then he let out a sigh and was still. Jo lay frozen beneath him, uncertain what had happened.

Damien dropped his pistol and collapsed against the ground, cursing with every breath he took. He realized his wound was severe, and that he was losing a tremendous amount of blood. He rolled onto his back and vainly tried to stanch the flow with his hands. In a moment or two he would be so weak he would be past the point of caring whether or not he bled to death. It was strange, he mused grimly, but somehow when he had come to the colonies he had not imagined his death would be at the hands of an Indian as he tried to save a simple farm girl.

"Are you all right, Jo?" demanded Samuel anxiously. He moved to where she lay buried beneath the dead warrior.

"I think so," she managed, her voice thin and trembling. "Help me get him off."

Samuel grabbed one of the Indian's arms and pulled. Jo pushed until the dead man's body moved enough for her to scramble out from underneath it. The minute she was free she rushed over to the injured man who had saved her life.

Her throat constricted in horror as she stared down at him. Numbly she took in the scarlet color of his torn jacket, the white waistcoat stained ruby with blood, and the filthy white of his breeches. "Oh dear Lord," she gasped, appalled. "You're a *redcoat*!"

Damien forced his eyes open to look at the woman who had cost him his life. Her eyes were the color of the sky, as clear and brilliant a shade of blue as he had ever seen. Her sunlit hair tumbled wildly over her shoulders, forming a golden veil of silk around her. *It was worth it*, he decided absently as pain clouded over his mind.

She did not move closer but continued to stare at him, her expression a mixture of wariness and fear. He frowned, wondering why she was afraid. And then her words pierced through the dark haze that had almost claimed his consciousness.

Christ, he thought as blackness drowned his senses.

A bloody patriot.

On sale in May:

VICE
by Jane Feather

THE ENGAGEMENT
by Suzanne Robinson

NIGHT MOVES
by Sandra Canfield

SWEET LOVE, SURVIVE
by Susan Johnson

OFFICIAL RULES **NO PURCHASE NECESSARY**

To enter the sweepstakes outlined below, you must respond by the date specified and follow all entry instructions published elsewhere in this offer.

DREAM COME TRUE SWEEPSTAKES

Sweepstakes begins 9/1/94, ends 1/15/96. To qualify for the Early Bird Prize, entry must be received by the date specified elsewhere in this offer. Winners will be selected in random drawings on 2/29/96 by an independent judging organization whose decisions are final. Early Bird winner will be selected in a separate drawing from among all qualifying entries.

Odds of winning determined by total number of entries received. Distribution not to exceed 300 million.

Estimated maximum retail value of prizes: Grand (1) $25,000 (cash alternative $20,000); First (1) $2,000; Second (1) $750; Third (50) $75; Fourth (1,000) $50; Early Bird (1) $5,000. Total prize value: $86,500.

Automobile and travel trailer must be picked up at a local dealer; all other merchandise prizes will be shipped to winners. Awarding of any prize to a minor will require written permission of parent/guardian. If a trip prize is won by a minor, s/he must be accompanied by parent/legal guardian. Trip prizes subject to availability and must be completed within 12 months of date awarded. Blackout dates may apply. Early Bird trip is on a space available basis and does not include port charges, gratuities, optional shore excursions and onboard personal purchases. Prizes are not transferable or redeemable for cash except as specified. No substitution for prizes except as necessary due to unavailability. Travel trailer and/or automobile license and registration fees are winners' responsibility as are any other incidental expenses not specified herein.

Early Bird Prize may not be offered in some presentations of this sweepstakes. Grand through third prize winners will have the option of selecting any prize offered at level won. All prizes will be awarded. Drawing will be held at 204 Center Square Road, Bridgeport, NJ 08014. Winners need not be present. For winners list (available in June, 1996), send a self-addressed, stamped envelope by 1/15/96 to: Dream Come True Winners, P.O. Box 572, Gibbstown, NJ 08027.

THE FOLLOWING APPLIES TO THE SWEEPSTAKES ABOVE:

No purchase necessary. No photocopied or mechanically reproduced entries will be accepted. Not responsible for lost, late, misdirected, damaged, incomplete, illegible, or postage-die mail. Entries become the property of sponsors and will not be returned.

Winner(s) will be notified by mail. Winner(s) may be required to sign and return an affidavit of eligibility/release within 14 days of date on notification or an alternate may be selected. Except where prohibited by law, entry constitutes permission to use of winners' names, hometowns, and likenesses for publicity without additional compensation. Void where prohibited or restricted. All federal, state, provincial, and local laws and regulations apply.

All prize values are in U.S. currency. Presentation of prizes may vary; values at a given prize level will be approximately the same. All taxes are winners' responsibility.

Canadian residents, in order to win, must first correctly answer a time-limited skill testing question administered by mail. Any litigation regarding the conduct and awarding of a prize in this publicity contest by a resident of the province of Quebec may be submitted to the Regie des loteries et courses du Quebec.

Sweepstakes is open to legal residents of the U.S., Canada, and Europe (in those areas where made available) who have received this offer.

Sweepstakes in sponsored by Ventura Associates, 1211 Avenue of the Americas, New York, NY 10036 and presented by independent businesses. Employees of these, their advertising agencies and promotional companies involved in this promotion, and their immediate families, agents, successors, and assignees shall be ineligible to participate in the promotion and shall not be eligible for any prizes covered herein. SWP 3/95